Oscar Wilde – The Duchess Of Padua

Includes a biography of the author.

THE PERSONS OF THE PLAY

Simone Gesso, Duke of Padua
Beatrice, his Wife
Andreas Pollajuolo, Cardinal of Padua
Maffio Petrucci, }
Jeppo Vitellozzo, } Gentlemen of the Duke's Household
Taddeo Bardi, }
Guido Ferranti, a Young Man
Ascanio Cristofano, his Friend
Count Moranzone, an Old Man
Bernardo Cavalcanti, Lord Justice of Padua
Hugo, the Headsman
Lucy, a Tire woman

Servants, Citizens, Soldiers, Monks, Falconers with their hawks and
dogs, etc.

Place: Padua
Time: The latter half of the Sixteenth Century
Style of Architecture: Italian, Gothic and Romanesque.

THE SCENES OF THE PLAY
ACT I. The Market Place of Padua (25 minutes).
ACT II. Room in the Duke's Palace (36 minutes).
ACT III. Corridor in the Duke's Palace (29 minutes).
ACT IV. The Hall of Justice (31 minutes).
ACT V. The Dungeon (25 minutes).

ACT I

SCENE

The Market Place of Padua at noon; in the background is the great
Cathedral of Padua; the architecture is Romanesque, and wrought in
black and white marbles; a flight of marble steps leads up to the
Cathedral door; at the foot of the steps are two large stone lions;
the houses on each aide of the stage have coloured awnings from
their windows, and are flanked by stone arcades; on the right of

the stage is the public fountain, with a triton in green bronze blowing from a conch; around the fountain is a stone seat; the bell of the Cathedral is ringing, and the citizens, men, women and children, are passing into the Cathedral.

[Enter GUIDO FERRANTI and ASCANIO CRISTOFANO.]

ASCANIO.
Now by my life, Guido, I will go no farther; for if I walk another step I will have no life left to swear by; this wild-goose errand of yours!

[Sits down on the step of the fountain.]

GUIDO.
I think it must be here. [Goes up to passer-by and doffs his cap.] Pray, sir, is this the market place, and that the church of Santa Croce? [Citizen bows.] I thank you, sir.

ASCANIO.
Well?

GUIDO.
Ay! it is here.

ASCANIO.
I would it were somewhere else, for I see no wine-shop.

GUIDO.
[Taking a letter from his pocket and reading it.] 'The hour noon; the city, Padua; the place, the market; and the day, Saint Philip's Day.'

ASCANIO.
And what of the man, how shall we know him?

GUIDO.
[reading still] 'I will wear a violet cloak with a silver falcon broidered on the shoulder.' A brave attire, Ascanio.

ASCANIO.
I'd sooner have my leathern jerkin. And you think he will tell you of your father?

GUIDO.
Why, yes! It is a month ago now, you remember; I was in the vineyard, just at the corner nearest the road, where the goats used to get in, a man rode up and asked me was my name Guido, and gave me this letter, signed 'Your Father's Friend,' bidding me be here to-day if I would know the secret of my birth, and telling me how to recognise the writer! I had always thought old Pedro was my

uncle, but he told me that he was not, but that I had been left a
child in his charge by some one he had never since seen.

ASCANIO.
And you don't know who your father is?

GUIDO.
No.

ASCANIO.
No recollection of him even?

GUIDO.
None, Ascanio, none.

ASCANIO.
[laughing] Then he could never have boxed your ears so often as my
father did mine.

GUIDO.
[smiling] I am sure you never deserved it.

ASCANIO.
Never; and that made it worse. I hadn't the consciousness of guilt
to buoy me up. What hour did you say he fixed?

GUIDO.
Noon. [Clock in the Cathedral strikes.]

ASCANIO.
It is that now, and your man has not come. I don't believe in him,
Guido. I think it is some wench who has set her eye at you; and,
as I have followed you from Perugia to Padua, I swear you shall
follow me to the nearest tavern. [Rises.] By the great gods of
eating, Guido, I am as hungry as a widow is for a husband, as tired
as a young maid is of good advice, and as dry as a monk's sermon.
Come, Guido, you stand there looking at nothing, like the fool who
tried to look into his own mind; your man will not come.

GUIDO.
Well, I suppose you are right. Ah! [Just as he is leaving the
stage with ASCANIO, enter LORD MORANZONE in a violet cloak, with a
silver falcon broidered on the shoulder; he passes across to the
Cathedral, and just as he is going in GUIDO runs up and touches
him.]

MORANZONE
Guido Ferranti, thou hast come in time.

GUIDO.
What! Does my father live?

MORANZONE
Ay! lives in thee.
Thou art the same in mould and lineament,
Carriage and form, and outward semblances;
I trust thou art in noble mind the same.

GUIDO.
Oh, tell me of my father; I have lived but for this moment.

MORANZONE
We must be alone.

GUIDO.

This is my dearest friend, who out of love
Has followed me to Padua; as two brothers,
There is no secret which we do not share.

MORANZONE
There is one secret which ye shall not share;
Bid him go hence.

GUIDO.
[to ASCANIO] Come back within the hour.
He does not know that nothing in this world
Can dim the perfect mirror of our love.
Within the hour come.

ASCANIO.
Speak not to him,
There is a dreadful terror in his look.

GUIDO.
[laughing]
Nay, nay, I doubt not that he has come to tell
That I am some great Lord of Italy,
And we will have long days of joy together.
Within the hour, dear Ascanio.
[Exit ASCANIO.]
Now tell me of my father?
[Sits down on a stone seat.]
Stood he tall?
I warrant he looked tall upon his horse.
His hair was black? or perhaps a reddish gold,
Like a red fire of gold? Was his voice low?
The very bravest men have voices sometimes
Full of low music; or a clarion was it
That brake with terror all his enemies?
Did he ride singly? or with many squires
And valiant gentlemen to serve his state?

For oftentimes methinks I feel my veins
Beat with the blood of kings. Was he a king?

MORANZONE
Ay, of all men he was the kingliest.

GUIDO.
[proudly] Then when you saw my noble father last
He was set high above the heads of men?

MORANZONE
Ay, he was high above the heads of men,
[Walks over to GUIDO and puts his hand upon his shoulder.]
On a red scaffold, with a butcher's block
Set for his neck.

GUIDO.
[leaping up]
What dreadful man art thou,
That like a raven, or the midnight owl,
Com'st with this awful message from the grave?

MORANZONE
I am known here as the Count MORANZONE,
Lord of a barren castle on a rock,
With a few acres of unkindly land
And six not thrifty SERVANTS. But I was one
Of Parma's noblest princes; more than that,
I was your father's friend.

GUIDO.
[clasping his hand] Tell me of him.

MORANZONE
You are the son of that great DUKE Lorenzo,
He was the Prince of Parma, and the DUKE
Of all the fair domains of Lombardy
Down to the gates of Florence; nay, Florence even
Was wont to pay him tribute -

GUIDO.
Come to his death.

MORANZONE
You will hear that soon enough. Being at war -
O noble lion of war, that would not suffer
Injustice done in Italy! he led
The very flower of chivalry against
That foul adulterous Lord of Rimini,
Giovanni Malatesta, whom God curse!
And was by him in treacherous ambush taken,

And like a villain, or a low-born knave,
Was by him on the public scaffold murdered.

GUIDO.
[clutching his dagger] Doth Malatesta live?

MORANZONE
No, he is dead.

GUIDO.
Did you say dead? O too swift runner, Death,
Couldst thou not wait for me a little space,
And I had done thy bidding!

MORANZONE
[clutching his wrist] Thou canst do it!
The man who sold thy father is alive.

GUIDO.
Sold! was my father sold?

MORANZONE
Ay! trafficked for,
Like a vile chattel, for a price betrayed,
Bartered and bargained for in privy market
By one whom he had held his perfect friend,
One he had trusted, one he had well loved,
One whom by ties of kindness he had bound -

GUIDO.
And he lives
Who sold my father?

MORANZONE
I will bring you to him.

GUIDO.
So, Judas, thou art living! well, I will make
This world thy field of blood, so buy it straight-way,
For thou must hang there.

MORANZONE
Judas said you, boy?
Yes, Judas in his treachery, but still
He was more wise than Judas was, and held
Those thirty silver pieces not enough.

GUIDO.
What got he for my father's blood?

MORANZONE

What got he?
Why cities, fiefs, and principalities,
Vineyards, and lands.

GUIDO.

Of which he shall but keep
Six feet of ground to rot in. Where is he,
This damned villain, this foul devil? where?
Show me the man, and come he cased in steel,
In complete panoply and pride of war,
Ay, guarded by a thousand men-at-arms,
Yet I shall reach him through their spears, and feel
The last black drop of blood from his black heart
Crawl down my blade. Show me the man, I say,
And I will kill him.

MORANZONE

[coldly]
Fool, what revenge is there?
Death is the common heritage of all,
And death comes best when it comes suddenly.
[Goes up close to GUIDO.]
Your father was betrayed, there is your cue;
For you shall sell the seller in his turn.
I will make you of his household, you shall sit
At the same board with him, eat of his bread -

GUIDO.

O bitter bread!

MORANZONE

Thy palate is too nice,
Revenge will make it sweet. Thou shalt o' nights
Pledge him in wine, drink from his cup, and be
His intimate, so he will fawn on thee,
Love thee, and trust thee in all secret things.
If he bid thee be merry thou must laugh,
And if it be his humour to be sad
Thou shalt don sables. Then when the time is ripe -
[GUIDO clutches his sword.]
Nay, nay, I trust thee not; your hot young blood,
Undisciplined nature, and too violent rage
Will never tarry for this great revenge,
But wreck itself on passion.

GUIDO.

Thou knowest me not.
Tell me the man, and I in everything
Will do thy bidding.

MORANZONE
Well, when the time is ripe,
The victim trusting and the occasion sure,
I will by sudden secret messenger
Send thee a sign.

GUIDO.
How shall I kill him, tell me?

MORANZONE
That night thou shalt creep into his private chamber;
But if he sleep see that thou wake him first,
And hold thy hand upon his throat, ay! that way,
Then having told him of what blood thou art,
Sprung from what father, and for what revenge,
Bid him to pray for mercy; when he prays,
Bid him to set a price upon his life,
And when he strips himself of all his gold
Tell him thou needest not gold, and hast not mercy,
And do thy business straight away. Swear to me
Thou wilt not kill him till I bid thee do it,
Or else I go to mine own house, and leave
Thee ignorant, and thy father unavenged.

GUIDO.
Now by my father's sword -

MORANZONE
The common hangman
Brake that in sunder in the public square.

GUIDO.
Then by my father's grave -

MORANZONE
What grave? what grave?
Your noble father lieth in no grave,
I saw his dust strewn on the air, his ashes
Whirled through the windy streets like common straws
To plague a beggar's eyesight, and his head,
That gentle head, set on the prison spike,
For the vile rabble in their insolence
To shoot their tongues at.

GUIDO.
Was it so indeed?
Then by my father's spotless memory,
And by the shameful manner of his death,
And by the base betrayal by his friend,
For these at least remain, by these I swear
I will not lay my hand upon his life

Until you bid me, then God help his soul,
For he shall die as never dog died yet.
And now, the sign, what is it?

MORANZONE
This dagger, boy;
It was your father's.

GUIDO.
Oh, let me look at it!
I do remember now my reputed uncle,
That good old husbandman I left at home,
Told me a cloak wrapped round me when a babe
Bare too such yellow leopards wrought in gold;
I like them best in steel, as they are here,
They suit my purpose better. Tell me, sir,
Have you no message from my father to me?

MORANZONE
Poor boy, you never saw that noble father,
For when by his false friend he had been sold,
Alone of all his gentlemen I escaped
To bear the news to Parma to the Duchess.

GUIDO.
Speak to me of my mother.

MORANZONE
When thy mother
Heard my black news, she fell into a swoon,
And, being with untimely travail seized -
Bare thee into the world before thy time,
And then her soul went heavenward, to wait
Thy father, at the gates of Paradise.

GUIDO.
A mother dead, a father sold and bartered!
I seem to stand on some beleaguered wall,
And messenger comes after messenger
With a new tale of terror; give me breath,
Mine ears are tired.

MORANZONE
When thy mother died,
Fearing our enemies, I gave it out
Thou wert dead also, and then privily
Conveyed thee to an ancient servitor,
Who by Perugia lived; the rest thou knowest.

GUIDO.
Saw you my father afterwards?

MORANZONE

Ay! once;
In mean attire, like a vineyard dresser,
I stole to Rimini.

GUIDO.

[taking his hand]
O generous heart!

MORANZONE

One can buy everything in Rimini,
And so I bought the gaolers! when your father
Heard that a man child had been born to him,
His noble face lit up beneath his helm
Like a great fire seen far out at sea,
And taking my two hands, he bade me, Guido,
To rear you worthy of him; so I have reared you
To revenge his death upon the friend who sold him.

GUIDO.

Thou hast done well; I for my father thank thee.
And now his name?

MORANZONE

How you remind me of him,
You have each gesture that your father had.

GUIDO.

The traitor's name?

MORANZONE

Thou wilt hear that anon;
The **DUKE** and other nobles at the Court
Are coming hither.

GUIDO.

What of that? his name?

MORANZONE

Do they not seem a valiant company
Of honourable, honest gentlemen?

GUIDO.

His name, milord?

[Enter the DUKE OF PADUA with COUNT BARDI, MAFFIO, PETRUCCI,
and other gentlemen of his Court.]

MORANZONE

[quickly]

The man to whom I kneel
Is he who sold your father! mark me well.

GUIDO.
[clutches hit dagger]
The DUKE!

MORANZONE
Leave off that fingering of thy knife.
Hast thou so soon forgotten?
[Kneels to the DUKE.]
My noble Lord.

DUKE
Welcome, Count MORANZONE; 'tis some time
Since we have seen you here in Padua.
We hunted near your castle yesterday -
Call you it castle? that bleak house of yours
Wherein you sit a-mumbling o'er your beads,
Telling your vices like a good old man.
[Catches sight of GUIDO and starts back.]
Who is that?

MORANZONE

My sister's son, your Grace,
Who being now of age to carry arms,
Would for a season tarry at your Court

DUKE
[still looking at GUIDO]
What is his name?

MORANZONE
Guido Ferranti, sir.

DUKE
His city?

MORANZONE
He is Mantuan by birth.

DUKE
[advancing towards GUIDO]
You have the eyes of one I used to know,
But he died childless. Are you honest, boy?
Then be not spendthrift of your honesty,
But keep it to yourself; in Padua
Men think that honesty is ostentatious, so
It is not of the fashion. Look at these lords.

COUNT BARDI
[aside]
Here is some bitter arrow for us, sure.

DUKE
Why, every man among them has his price,
Although, to do them justice, some of them
Are quite expensive.

COUNT BARDI
[aside]
There it comes indeed.

DUKE
So be not honest; eccentricity
Is not a thing should ever be encouraged,
Although, in this dull stupid age of ours,
The most eccentric thing a man can do
Is to have brains, then the mob mocks at him;
And for the mob, despise it as I do,
I hold its bubble praise and windy favours
In such account, that popularity
Is the one insult I have never suffered.

MAFFIO
[aside]
He has enough of hate, if he needs that.

DUKE
Have prudence; in your dealings with the world
Be not too hasty; act on the second thought,
First impulses are generally good.

GUIDO.
[aside]
Surely a toad sits on his lips, and spills its venom there.

DUKE
See thou hast enemies,
Else will the world think very little of thee;
It is its test of power; yet see thou show'st
A smiling mask of friendship to all men,
Until thou hast them safely in thy grip,
Then thou canst crush them.

GUIDO.
[aside]
O wise philosopher!
That for thyself dost dig so deep a grave.

MORANZONE
[to him]
Dost thou mark his words?

GUIDO.
Oh, be thou sure I do.

DUKE
And be not over-scrupulous; clean hands
With nothing in them make a sorry show.
If you would have the lion's share of life
You must wear the fox's skin. Oh, it will fit you;
It is a coat which fitteth every man.

GUIDO.
Your Grace, I shall remember.

DUKE
That is well, boy, well.
I would not have about me shallow fools,
Who with mean scruples weigh the gold of life,
And faltering, paltering, end by failure; failure,
The only crime which I have not committed:
I would have MEN about me. As for conscience,
Conscience is but the name which cowardice
Fleeing from battle scrawls upon its shield.
You understand me, boy?

GUIDO.
I do, your Grace,
And will in all things carry out the creed
Which you have taught me.

MAFFIO
I never heard your Grace
So much in the vein for preaching; let the **CARDINAL**
Look to his laurels, sir.

DUKE
The CARDINAL!
Men follow my creed, and they gabble his.
I do not think much of the **CARDINAL** ;
Although he is a holy churchman, and
I quite admit his dulness. Well, sir, from now
We count you of our household
[He holds out his hand for GUIDO to kiss. GUIDO starts
back in horror, but at a gesture from COUNT MORANZONE,
kneels and kisses it.]
We will see
That you are furnished with such equipage
As doth befit your honour and our state.

GUIDO.
I thank your Grace most heartily.

DUKE
Tell me again
What is your name?

GUIDO.
Guido Ferranti, sir.

DUKE
And you are Mantuan? Look to your wives, my lords,
When such a gallant comes to Padua.
Thou dost well to laugh, COUNT BARDI; I have noted
How merry is that husband by whose hearth
Sits an uncomely wife.

MAFFIO
May it please your Grace,
The wives of Padua are above suspicion.

DUKE
What, are they so ill-favoured! Let us go,
This CARDINAL detains our pious Duchess;
His sermon and his beard want cutting both:
Will you come with us, sir, and hear a text
From holy Jerome?

MORANZONE
[bowing]
My liege, there are some matters -

DUKE
[interrupting]
Thou need'st make no excuse for missing mass.
Come, gentlemen.
[Exit with his suite into Cathedral.]

GUIDO.
[after a pause]
So the DUKE sold my father;
I kissed his hand.

MORANZONE
Thou shalt do that many times.

GUIDO.
Must it be so?

MORANZONE
Ay! thou hast sworn an oath.

GUIDO.
That oath shall make me marble.

MORANZONE
Farewell, boy,
Thou wilt not see me till the time is ripe.

GUIDO.
I pray thou comest quickly.

MORANZONE
I will come
When it is time; be ready.

GUIDO.
Fear me not.

MORANZONE
Here is your friend; see that you banish him
Both from your heart and Padua.

GUIDO.
From Padua,
Not from my heart.

MORANZONE
Nay, from thy heart as well,
I will not leave thee till I see thee do it.

GUIDO.
Can I have no friend?

MORANZONE
Revenge shall be thy friend;
Thou need'st no other.

GUIDO.
Well, then be it so.
[Enter ASCANIO CRISTOFANO.]

ASCANIO.
Come, Guido, I have been beforehand with you in everything, for I
have drunk a flagon of wine, eaten a pasty, and kissed the maid who
served it. Why, you look as melancholy as a schoolboy who cannot
buy apples, or a politician who cannot sell his vote. What news,
Guido, what news?

GUIDO.
Why, that we two must part, Ascanio.

ASCANIO.
That would be news indeed, but it is not true.

GUIDO.
Too true it is, you must get hence, Ascanio,
And never look upon my face again.

ASCANIO.
No, no; indeed you do not know me, Guido;
'Tis true I am a common yeoman's son,
Nor versed in fashions of much courtesy;
But, if you are nobly born, cannot I be
Your serving man? I will tend you with more love
Than any hired SERVANT.

GUIDO.
[clasping his hand]
Ascanio!
[Sees **MORANZONE** looking at him and drops ASCANIO'S hand.]
It cannot be.

ASCANIO.
What, is it so with you?
I thought the friendship of the antique world
Was not yet dead, but that the Roman type
Might even in this poor and common age
Find counterparts of love; then by this love
Which beats between us like a summer sea,
Whatever lot has fallen to your hand
May I not share it?

GUIDO.
Share it?

ASCANIO.
Ay!

GUIDO.
No, no.

ASCANIO.
Have you then come to some inheritance
Of lordly castle, or of stored-up gold?

GUIDO.
[bitterly]
Ay! I have come to my inheritance.
O bloody legacy! and O murderous dole!
Which, like the thrifty miser, must I hoard,
And to my own self keep; and so, I pray you,
Let us part here.

ASCANIO.
What, shall we never more
Sit hand in hand, as we were wont to sit,
Over some book of ancient chivalry
Stealing a truant holiday from school,
Follow the huntsmen through the autumn woods,
And watch the falcons burst their tasselled jesses,
When the hare breaks from covert.

GUIDO.
Never more.

ASCANIO.
Must I go hence without a word of love?

GUIDO.
You must go hence, and may love go with you.

ASCANIO.
You are unknightly, and ungenerous.

GUIDO.
Unknightly and ungenerous if you will.
Why should we waste more words about the matter
Let us part now.

ASCANIO.
Have you no message, Guido?

GUIDO.
None; my whole past was but a schoolboy's dream;
To-day my life begins. Farewell.

ASCANIO.
Farewell [exit slowly.]

GUIDO.
Now are you satisfied? Have you not seen
My dearest friend, and my most loved companion,
Thrust from me like a common kitchen knave!
Oh, that I did it! Are you not satisfied?

MORANZONE
Ay! I am satisfied. Now I go hence,
Do not forget the sign, your father's dagger,
And do the business when I send it to you.

GUIDO.
Be sure I shall. [Exit LORD MORANZONE.]

GUIDO.
O thou eternal heaven!
If there is aught of nature in my soul,
Of gentle pity, or fond kindliness,
Wither it up, blast it, bring it to nothing,
Or if thou wilt not, then will I myself
Cut pity with a sharp knife from my heart
And strangle mercy in her sleep at night
Lest she speak to me. Vengeance there I have it.
Be thou my comrade and my bedfellow,
Sit by my side, ride to the chase with me,
When I am weary sing me pretty songs,
When I am light o' heart, make jest with me,
And when I dream, whisper into my ear
The dreadful secret of a father's murder -
Did I say murder? [Draws his dagger.]
Listen, thou terrible God!
Thou God that punishest all broken oaths,
And bid some angel write this oath in fire,
That from this hour, till my dear father's murder
In blood I have revenged, I do forswear
The noble ties of honourable friendship,
The noble joys of dear companionship,
Affection's bonds, and loyal gratitude,
Ay, more, from this same hour I do forswear
All love of women, and the barren thing
Which men call beauty -
[The organ peals in the Cathedral, and under a canopy of cloth of
silver tissue, borne by four pages in scarlet, the DUCHESS OF PADUA
comes down the steps; as she passes across their eyes meet for a
moment, and as she leaves the stage she looks back at GUIDO, and
the dagger falls from his hand.]
Oh! who is that?

A CITIZEN
The Duchess of Padua!

END OF ACT I.

ACT II

SCENE

A state room in the Ducal Palace, hung with tapestries representing
the Masque of Venus; a large door in the centre opens into a
corridor of red marble, through which one can see a view of Padua;
a large canopy is set (R.C.) with three thrones, one a little lower
than the others; the ceiling is made of long gilded beams;
furniture of the period, chairs covered with gilt leather, and

buffets set with gold and silver plate, and chests painted with
mythological scenes. A number of the courtiers is out on the
corridor looking from it down into the street below; from the
street comes the roar of a mob and cries of 'Death to the DUKE':
after a little interval enter the DUKE very calmly; he is leaning
on the arm of Guido Ferranti; with him enters also the Lord
CARDINAL; the mob still shouting.

DUKE
No, my Lord CARDINAL, I weary of her!
Why, she is worse than ugly, she is good.

MAFFIO
[excitedly]
Your Grace, there are two thousand people there
Who every moment grow more clamorous.

DUKE
Tut, man, they waste their strength upon their lungs!
People who shout so loud, my lords, do nothing;
The only men I fear are silent men.
[A yell from the people.]
You see, Lord CARDINAL, how my people love me.
[Another yell.] Go, Petrucci,
And tell the captain of the guard below
To clear the square. Do you not hear me, sir?
Do what I bid you.

[Exit PETRUCCI.]

CARDINAL
I beseech your Grace
To listen to their grievances.

DUKE
[sitting on his throne]
Ay! the peaches
Are not so big this year as they were last.
I crave your pardon, my lord CARDINAL,
I thought you spake of peaches.
[A cheer from the people.]
What is that?

GUIDO.
[rushes to the window]
The Duchess has gone forth into the square,
And stands between the people and the guard,
And will not let them shoot.

DUKE
The devil take her!

GUIDO.
[still at the window]
And followed by a dozen of the citizens
Has come into the Palace.

DUKE
[starting up]
By Saint James,
Our Duchess waxes bold!

BARDI
Here comes the Duchess.

DUKE
Shut that door there; this morning air is cold.
[They close the door on the corridor.]
[Enter the Duchess followed by a crowd of meanly dressed Citizens.]

DUCHESS.
[flinging herself upon her knees]
I do beseech your Grace to give us audience.

DUKE
What are these grievances?

DUCHESS.
Alas, my Lord,
Such common things as neither you nor I,
Nor any of these noble gentlemen,
Have ever need at all to think about;
They say the bread, the very bread they eat,
Is made of sorry chaff.

FIRST CITIZEN
Ay! so it is,
Nothing but chaff.

DUKE
And very good food too,
I give it to my horses.

DUCHESS.
[restraining herself]
They say the water,
Set in the public cisterns for their use,
[Has, through the breaking of the aqueduct,]
To stagnant pools and muddy puddles turned.

DUKE
They should drink wine; water is quite unwholesome.

SECOND CITIZEN
Alack, your Grace, the taxes which the customs
Take at the city gate are grown so high
We cannot buy wine.

DUKE
Then you should bless the taxes
Which make you temperate.

DUCHESS.
Think, while we sit
In gorgeous pomp and state, gaunt poverty
Creeps through their sunless lanes, and with sharp knives
Cuts the warm throats of children stealthily
And no word said.

THIRD CITIZEN
Ay! marry, that is true,
My little son died yesternight from hunger;
He was but six years old; I am so poor,
I cannot bury him.

DUKE
If you are poor,
Are you not blessed in that? Why, poverty
Is one of the Christian virtues,
[Turns to the CARDINAL.]
Is it not?
I know, Lord CARDINAL, you have great revenues,
Rich abbey-lands, and tithes, and large estates
For preaching voluntary poverty.

DUCHESS.
Nay but, my lord the DUKE, be generous;
While we sit here within a noble house
[With shaded porticoes against the sun,
And walls and roofs to keep the winter out],
There are many citizens of Padua
Who in vile tenements live so full of holes,
That the chill rain, the snow, and the rude blast,
Are tenants also with them; others sleep
Under the arches of the public bridges
All through the autumn nights, till the wet mist
Stiffens their limbs, and fevers come, and so -

DUKE
And so they go to Abraham's bosom, Madam.
They should thank me for sending them to Heaven,
If they are wretched here.
[To the CARDINAL.]
Is it not said

Somewhere in Holy Writ, that every man
Should be contented with that state of life
God calls him to? Why should I change their state,
Or meddle with an all-wise providence,
Which has apportioned that some men should starve,
And others surfeit? I did not make the world.

FIRST CITIZEN
He hath a hard heart.

SECOND CITIZEN
Nay, be silent, neighbour;
I think the CARDINAL will speak for us.

CARDINAL
True, it is Christian to bear misery,
Yet it is Christian also to be kind,
And there seem many evils in this town,
Which in your wisdom might your Grace reform.

FIRST CITIZEN

What is that word reform? What does it mean?

SECOND CITIZEN
Marry, it means leaving things as they are; I like it not.

DUKE
Reform Lord CARDINAL, did YOU say reform?
There is a man in Germany called Luther,
Who would reform the Holy Catholic Church.
Have you not made him heretic, and uttered
Anathema, maranatha, against him?

CARDINAL
[rising from his seat]
He would have led the sheep out of the fold,
We do but ask of you to feed the sheep.

DUKE
When I have shorn their fleeces I may feed them.
As for these rebels -
[DUCHESS entreats him.]

FIRST CITIZEN
That is a kind word,
He means to give us something.

SECOND CITIZEN
Is that so?

DUKE

These ragged knaves who come before us here,
With mouths chock-full of treason.

THIRD CITIZEN

Good my Lord,
Fill up our mouths with bread; we'll hold our tongues.

DUKE

Ye shall hold your tongues, whether you starve or not.
My lords, this age is so familiar grown,
That the low peasant hardly doffs his hat,
Unless you beat him; and the raw mechanic
Elbows the noble in the public streets.
[To the Citizens.]
Still as our gentle Duchess has so prayed us,
And to refuse so beautiful a beggar
Were to lack both courtesy and love,
Touching your grievances, I promise this -

FIRST CITIZEN

Marry, he will lighten the taxes!

SECOND CITIZEN

Or a dole of bread, think you, for each man?

DUKE

That, on next Sunday, the Lord CARDINAL
Shall, after Holy Mass, preach you a sermon
Upon the Beauty of Obedience.
[Citizens murmur.]

FIRST CITIZEN

I' faith, that will not fill our stomachs!

SECOND CITIZEN

A sermon is but a sorry sauce, when
You have nothing to eat with it.

DUCHESS. Poor people,
You see I have no power with the **DUKE** ,
But if you go into the court without,
My almoner shall from my private purse,
Divide a hundred ducats 'mongst you all.

FIRST CITIZEN

God save the Duchess, say I.

SECOND CITIZEN

God save her.

DUCHESS.
And every Monday morn shall bread be set
For those who lack it.
[Citizens applaud and go out.]

FIRST CITIZEN
[going out]
Why, God save the Duchess again!

DUKE
[calling him back]
Come hither, fellow! what is your name?

FIRST CITIZEN
Dominick, sir.

DUKE
A good name! Why were you called Dominick?

FIRST CITIZEN
[scratching his head]
Marry, because I was born on St. George's day.

DUKE
A good reason! here is a ducat for you!
Will you not cry for me God save the **DUKE** ?

FIRST CITIZEN
[feebly]
God save the DUKE.

DUKE
Nay! louder, fellow, louder.

FIRST CITIZEN
[a little louder]
God save the DUKE!

DUKE
More lustily, fellow, put more heart in it!
Here is another ducat for you.

FIRST CITIZEN
[enthusiastically]
God save the DUKE!

DUKE
[mockingly]
Why, gentlemen, this simple fellow's love
Touches me much. [To the Citizen, harshly.]
Go! [Exit Citizen, bowing.]

This is the way, my lords,
You can buy popularity nowadays.
Oh, we are nothing if not democratic!
[To the DUCHESS.]
Well, Madam,
You spread rebellion 'midst our citizens.

DUCHESS.
My Lord, the poor have rights you cannot touch,
The right to pity, and the right to mercy.

DUKE
So, so, you argue with me? This is she,
The gentle Duchess for whose hand I yielded
Three of the fairest towns in Italy,
Pisa, and Genoa, and Orvieto.

DUCHESS.
Promised, my Lord, not yielded: in that matter
Brake you your word as ever.

DUKE
You wrong us, Madam,
There were state reasons.

DUCHESS.
What state reasons are there
For breaking holy promises to a state?

DUKE
There are wild boars at Pisa in a forest
Close to the city: when I promised Pisa
Unto your noble and most trusting father,
I had forgotten there was hunting there.
At Genoa they say,
Indeed I doubt them not, that the red mullet
Runs larger in the harbour of that town
Than anywhere in Italy.
[Turning to one of the Court.]
You, my lord,
Whose gluttonous appetite is your only god,
Could satisfy our Duchess on that point.

DUCHESS.
And Orvieto?

DUKE
[yawning]
I cannot now recall
Why I did not surrender Orvieto
According to the word of my contract.

Maybe it was because I did not choose.
[Goes over to the DUCHESS.]
Why look you, Madam, you are here alone;
'Tis many a dusty league to your grey France,
And even there your father barely keeps
A hundred ragged squires for his Court.
What hope have you, I say? Which of these lords
And noble gentlemen of Padua
Stands by your side.

DUCHESS.

There is not one.

[GUIDO starts, but restrains himself.]

DUKE

Nor shall be,
While I am DUKE in Padua: listen, Madam,
Being mine own, you shall do as I will,
And if it be my will you keep the house,
Why then, this palace shall your prison be;
And if it be my will you walk abroad,
Why, you shall take the air from morn to night.

DUCHESS.

Sir, by what right -?

DUKE

Madam, my second Duchess
Asked the same question once: her monument
Lies in the chapel of Bartholomew,
Wrought in red marble; very beautiful.
Guido, your arm. Come, gentlemen, let us go
And spur our falcons for the mid-day chase.
Bethink you, Madam, you are here alone.
[Exit the **DUKE** leaning on GUIDO, with his Court.]

DUCHESS.

[looking after them]
The DUKE said rightly that I was alone;
Deserted, and dishonoured, and defamed,
Stood ever woman so alone indeed?
Men when they woo us call us pretty children,
Tell us we have not wit to make our lives,
And so they mar them for us. Did I say woo?
We are their chattels, and their common slaves,
Less dear than the poor hound that licks their hand,
Less fondled than the hawk upon their wrist.
Woo, did I say? bought rather, sold and bartered,
Our very bodies being merchandise.
I know it is the general lot of women,

Each miserably mated to some man
Wrecks her own life upon his selfishness:
That it is general makes it not less bitter.
I think I never heard a woman laugh,
Laugh for pure merriment, except one woman,
That was at night time, in the public streets.
Poor soul, she walked with painted lips, and wore
The mask of pleasure: I would not laugh like her;
No, death were better.
[Enter GUIDO behind unobserved; the DUCHESS flings herself down
before a picture of the Madonna.]
O Mary mother, with your sweet pale face
Bending between the little angel heads
That hover round you, have you no help for me?
Mother of God, have you no help for me?

GUIDO.
I can endure no longer.
This is my love, and I will speak to her.
Lady, am I a stranger to your prayers?

DUCHESS.
[rising]
None but the wretched needs my prayers, my lord.

GUIDO.
Then must I need them, lady.

DUCHESS.
How is that?
Does not the DUKE show thee sufficient honour?

GUIDO.
Your Grace, I lack no favours from the **DUKE** ,
Whom my soul loathes as I loathe wickedness,
But come to proffer on my bended knees,
My loyal service to thee unto death.

DUCHESS.
Alas! I am so fallen in estate
I can but give thee a poor meed of thanks.

GUIDO.
[seizing her hand]
Hast thou no love to give me?
[The DUCHESS starts, and GUIDO falls at her feet.]
O dear saint,
If I have been too daring, pardon me!
Thy beauty sets my boyish blood aflame,
And, when my reverent lips touch thy white hand,
Each little nerve with such wild passion thrills

That there is nothing which I would not do
To gain thy love. [Leaps up.]
Bid me reach forth and pluck
Perilous honour from the lion's jaws,
And I will wrestle with the Nemean beast
On the bare desert! Fling to the cave of War
A gaud, a ribbon, a dead flower, something
That once has touched thee, and I'll bring it back
Though all the hosts of Christendom were there,
Inviolate again! ay, more than this,
Set me to scale the pallid white-faced cliffs
Of mighty England, and from that arrogant shield
Will I raze out the lilies of your France
Which England, that sea-lion of the sea,
Hath taken from her!
O dear Beatrice,
Drive me not from thy presence! without thee
The heavy minutes crawl with feet of lead,
But, while I look upon thy loveliness,
The hours fly like winged Mercuries
And leave existence golden.

DUCHESS.
I did not think
I should be ever loved: do you indeed
Love me so much as now you say you do?

GUIDO.
Ask of the sea-bird if it loves the sea,
Ask of the roses if they love the rain,
Ask of the little lark, that will not sing
Till day break, if it loves to see the day:-
And yet, these are but empty images,
Mere shadows of my love, which is a fire
So great that all the waters of the main
Can not avail to quench it. Will you not speak?

DUCHESS.
I hardly know what I should say to you.

GUIDO.
Will you not say you love me?

DUCHESS.
Is that my lesson?
Must I say all at once? 'Twere a good lesson
If I did love you, sir; but, if I do not,
What shall I say then?

GUIDO.
If you do not love me,

Say, none the less, you do, for on your tongue
Falsehood for very shame would turn to truth.

DUCHESS.
What if I do not speak at all? They say
Lovers are happiest when they are in doubt

GUIDO.
Nay, doubt would kill me, and if I must die,
Why, let me die for joy and not for doubt.
Oh, tell me may I stay, or must I go?

DUCHESS.
I would not have you either stay or go;
For if you stay you steal my love from me,
And if you go you take my love away.
Guido, though all the morning stars could sing
They could not tell the measure of my love.
I love you, Guido.

GUIDO.
[stretching out his hands]
Oh, do not cease at all;
I thought the nightingale sang but at night;
Or if thou needst must cease, then let my lips
Touch the sweet lips that can such music make.

DUCHESS.
To touch my lips is not to touch my heart.

GUIDO.
Do you close that against me?

DUCHESS.
Alas! my lord,
I have it not: the first day that I saw you
I let you take my heart away from me;
Unwilling thief, that without meaning it
Did break into my fenced treasury
And filch my jewel from it! O strange theft,
Which made you richer though you knew it not,
And left me poorer, and yet glad of it!

GUIDO.
[clasping her in his arms]
O love, love, love! Nay, sweet, lift up your head,
Let me unlock those little scarlet doors
That shut in music, let me dive for coral
In your red lips, and I'll bear back a prize
Richer than all the gold the Gryphon guards
In rude Armenia.

DUCHESS.

You are my lord,
And what I have is yours, and what I have not
Your fancy lends me, like a prodigal
Spending its wealth on what is nothing worth.
[Kisses him.]

GUIDO.

Methinks I am bold to look upon you thus:
The gentle violet hides beneath its leaf
And is afraid to look at the great sun
For fear of too much splendour, but my eyes,
O daring eyes! are grown so venturous
That like fixed stars they stand, gazing at you,
And surfeit sense with beauty.

DUCHESS.

Dear love, I would
You could look upon me ever, for your eyes
Are polished mirrors, and when I peer
Into those mirrors I can see myself,
And so I know my image lives in you.

GUIDO.

[taking her in his arms]
Stand still, thou hurrying orb in the high heavens,
And make this hour immortal! [A pause.]

DUCHESS.

Sit down here,
A little lower than me: yes, just so, sweet,
That I may run my fingers through your hair,
And see your face turn upwards like a flower
To meet my kiss.
Have you not sometimes noted,
When we unlock some long-disused room
With heavy dust and soiling mildew filled,
Where never foot of man has come for years,
And from the windows take the rusty bar,
And fling the broken shutters to the air,
And let the bright sun in, how the good sun
Turns every grimy particle of dust
Into a little thing of dancing gold?
Guido, my heart is that long-empty room,
But you have let love in, and with its gold
Gilded all life. Do you not think that love
Fills up the sum of life?

GUIDO.

Ay! without love
Life is no better than the unhewn stone

Which in the quarry lies, before the sculptor
Has set the God within it. Without love
Life is as silent as the common reeds
That through the marshes or by rivers grow,
And have no music in them.

DUCHESS.
Yet out of these
The singer, who is Love, will make a pipe
And from them he draws music; so I think
Love will bring music out of any life.
Is that not true?

GUIDO.
Sweet, women make it true.
There are men who paint pictures, and carve statues,
Paul of Verona and the dyer's son,
Or their great rival, who, by the sea at Venice,
Has set God's little maid upon the stair,
White as her own white lily, and as tall,
Or Raphael, whose Madonnas are divine
Because they are mothers merely; yet I think
Women are the best artists of the world,
For they can take the common lives of men
Soiled with the money-getting of our age,
And with love make them beautiful.

DUCHESS.
Ah, dear,
I wish that you and I were very poor;
The poor, who love each other, are so rich.

GUIDO.
Tell me again you love me, Beatrice.

DUCHESS.
[fingering his collar]
How well this collar lies about your throat.
[LORD MORANZONE looks through the door from the corridor outside.]

GUIDO.
Nay, tell me that you love me.

DUCHESS.I remember,
That when I was a child in my dear France,
Being at Court at Fontainebleau, the King
Wore such a collar.

GUIDO. Will you not say you love me?

DUCHESS.
[smiling]
He was a very royal man, King Francis,
Yet he was not royal as you are.
Why need I tell you, Guido, that I love you?
[Takes his head in her hands and turns his face up to her.]
Do you not know that I am yours for ever,
Body and soul?
[Kisses him, and then suddenly catches sight of MORANZONE
and leaps up.]
Oh, what is that? [MORANZONE disappears.]

GUIDO.
What, love?

DUCHESS.
Methought I saw a face with eyes of flame
Look at us through the doorway.

GUIDO.
Nay, 'twas nothing:
The passing shadow of the man on guard.
[The DUCHESS still stands looking at the window.]
'Twas nothing, sweet.

DUCHESS.
Ay! what can harm us now,
Who are in Love's hand? I do not think I'd care
Though the vile world should with its lackey Slander
Trample and tread upon my life; why should I?
They say the common field-flowers of the field
Have sweeter scent when they are trodden on
Than when they bloom alone, and that some herbs
Which have no perfume, on being bruised die
With all Arabia round them; so it is
With the young lives this dull world seeks to crush,
It does but bring the sweetness out of them,
And makes them lovelier often. And besides,
While we have love we have the best of life:
Is it not so?

GUIDO.
Dear, shall we play or sing?
I think that I could sing now.

DUCHESS.
Do not speak,
For there are times when all existences
Seem narrowed to one single ecstasy,
And Passion sets a seal upon the lips.

GUIDO.

Oh, with mine own lips let me break that seal!
You love me, Beatrice?

DUCHESS.

Ay! is it not strange
I should so love mine enemy?

GUIDO.

Who is he?

DUCHESS.

Why, you: that with your shaft did pierce my heart!
Poor heart, that lived its little lonely life
Until it met your arrow.

GUIDO.

Ah, dear love,
I am so wounded by that bolt myself
That with untended wounds I lie a-dying,
Unless you cure me, dear Physician.

DUCHESS.

I would not have you cured; for I am sick
With the same malady.

GUIDO.

Oh, how I love you!
See, I must steal the cuckoo's voice, and tell
The one tale over.

DUCHESS.

Tell no other tale!
For, if that is the little cuckoo's song,
The nightingale is hoarse, and the loud lark
Has lost its music.

GUIDO.

Kiss me, Beatrice!
[She takes his face in her hands and bends down and kisses him; a
loud knocking then comes at the door, and GUIDO leaps up; enter a
SERVANT.]

SERVANT

A package for you, sir.

GUIDO.

[carelessly] Ah! give it to me. SERVANT hands package wrapped in
vermilion silk, and exit; as GUIDO is about to open it the DUCHESS
comes up behind, and in sport takes it from him.]

DUCHESS.
[laughing]
Now I will wager it is from some girl
Who would have you wear her favour; I am so jealous
I will not give up the least part in you,
But like a miser keep you to myself,
And spoil you perhaps in keeping.

GUIDO.
It is nothing.

DUCHESS.
Nay, it is from some girl.

GUIDO.
You know 'tis not.

DUCHESS.
[turns her back and opens it]
Now, traitor, tell me what does this sign mean,
A dagger with two leopards wrought in steel?

GUIDO.
[taking it from her] O God!

DUCHESS.
I'll from the window look, and try
If I can't see the porter's livery
Who left it at the gate! I will not rest
Till I have learned your secret.
[Runs laughing into the corridor.]

GUIDO.
Oh, horrible!
Had I so soon forgot my father's death,
Did I so soon let love into my heart,
And must I banish love, and let in murder
That beats and clamours at the outer gate?
Ay, that I must! Have I not sworn an oath?
Yet not to-night; nay, it must be to-night.
Farewell then all the joy and light of life,
All dear recorded memories, farewell,
Farewell all love! Could I with bloody hands
Fondle and paddle with her innocent hands?
Could I with lips fresh from this butchery
Play with her lips? Could I with murderous eyes
Look in those violet eyes, whose purity
Would strike men blind, and make each eyeball reel
In night perpetual? No, murder has set
A barrier between us far too high
For us to kiss across it.

DUCHESS.
Guido!

GUIDO.
Beatrice,
You must forget that name, and banish me
Out of your life for ever.

DUCHESS.
[going towards him]
O dear love!

GUIDO.
[stepping back]
There lies a barrier between us two
We dare not pass.

DUCHESS.
I dare do anything
So that you are beside me.

GUIDO.
Ah! There it is,
I cannot be beside you, cannot breathe
The air you breathe; I cannot any more
Stand face to face with beauty, which unnerves
My shaking heart, and makes my desperate hand
Fail of its purpose Let me go hence, I pray;
Forget you ever looked upon me.

DUCHESS.
What!
With your hot kisses fresh upon my lips
Forget the vows of love you made to me?

GUIDO.
I take them back.

DUCHESS.
Alas, you cannot, Guido,
For they are part of nature now; the air
Is tremulous with their music, and outside
The little birds sing sweeter for those vows.

GUIDO.
There lies a barrier between us now,
Which then I knew not, or I had forgot.

DUCHESS.
There is no barrier, Guido; why, I will go

In poor attire, and will follow you
Over the world.

GUIDO.
[wildly]
The world's not wide enough
To hold us two! Farewell, farewell for ever.

DUCHESS.
[calm, and controlling her passion]
Why did you come into my life at all, then,
Or in the desolate garden of my heart
Sow that white flower of love -?

GUIDO.
O Beatrice!

DUCHESS.
Which now you would dig up, uproot, tear out,
Though each small fibre doth so hold my heart
That if you break one, my heart breaks with it?
Why did you come into my life? Why open
The secret wells of love I had sealed up?
Why did you open them -?

GUIDO.
O God!

DUCHESS.
[clenching her hand]
And let
The floodgates of my passion swell and burst
Till, like the wave when rivers overflow
That sweeps the forest and the farm away,
Love in the splendid avalanche of its might
Swept my life with it? Must I drop by drop
Gather these waters back and seal them up?
Alas! Each drop will be a tear, and so
Will with its saltness make life very bitter.

GUIDO.
I pray you speak no more, for I must go
Forth from your life and love, and make a way
On which you cannot follow.

DUCHESS.
I have heard
That sailors dying of thirst upon a raft,
Poor castaways upon a lonely sea,
Dream of green fields and pleasant water-courses,
And then wake up with red thirst in their throats,

And die more miserably because sleep
Has cheated them: so they die cursing sleep
For having sent them dreams: I will not curse you
Though I am cast away upon the sea
Which men call Desolation.

GUIDO.
O God, God!

DUCHESS.
But you will stay: listen, I love you, Guido.
[She waits a little.]
Is echo dead, that when I say I love you
There is no answer?

GUIDO.

Everything is dead,
Save one thing only, which shall die to-night!

DUCHESS.
If you are going, touch me not, but go.
[Exit GUIDO.]
Barrier! Barrier!
Why did he say there was a barrier?
There is no barrier between us two.
He lied to me, and shall I for that reason
Loathe what I love, and what I worshipped, hate?
I think we women do not love like that.
For if I cut his image from my heart,
My heart would, like a bleeding pilgrim, follow
That image through the world, and call it back
With little cries of love.
[Enter DUKE equipped for the chase, with falconers and hounds.]

DUKE
Madam, you keep us waiting;
You keep my dogs waiting.

DUCHESS.
I will not ride to-day.

DUKE
How now, what's this?

DUCHESS.
My Lord, I cannot go.

DUKE
What, pale face, do you dare to stand against me?
Why, I could set you on a sorry jade

And lead you through the town, till the low rabble
You feed toss up their hats and mock at you.

DUCHESS.

Have you no word of kindness ever for me?

DUKE

I hold you in the hollow of my hand
And have no need on you to waste kind words.

DUCHESS.

Well, I will go.

DUKE

[slapping his boot with his whip]
No, I have changed my mind,
You will stay here, and like a faithful wife
Watch from the window for our coming back.
Were it not dreadful if some accident
By chance should happen to your loving Lord?
Come, gentlemen, my hounds begin to chafe,
And I chafe too, having a patient wife.
Where is young Guido?

MAFFIO

My liege, I have not seen him
For a full hour past.

DUKE

It matters not,
I dare say I shall see him soon enough.
Well, Madam, you will sit at home and spin.
I do protest, sirs, the domestic virtues
Are often very beautiful in others.

[Exit DUKE with his Court.]

DUCHESS.

The stars have fought against me, that is all,
And thus to-night when my Lord lieth asleep,
Will I fall upon my dagger, and so cease.
My heart is such a stone nothing can reach it
Except the dagger's edge: let it go there,
To find what name it carries: ay! to-night
Death will divorce the **DUKE** ; and yet to-night
He may die also, he is very old.
Why should he not die? Yesterday his hand
Shook with a palsy: men have died from palsy,
And why not he? Are there not fevers also,
Agues and chills, and other maladies
Most incident to old age?

No, no, he will not die, he is too sinful;
Honest men die before their proper time.
Good men will die: men by whose side the **DUKE**
In all the sick pollution of his life
Seems like a leper: women and children die,
But the DUKE will not die, he is too sinful.
Oh, can it be
There is some immortality in sin,
Which virtue has not? And does the wicked man
Draw life from what to other men were death,
Like poisonous plants that on corruption live?
No, no, I think God would not suffer that:
Yet the DUKE will not die: he is too sinful.
But I will die alone, and on this night
Grim Death shall be my bridegroom, and the tomb
My secret house of pleasure: well, what of that?
The world's a graveyard, and we each, like coffins,
Within us bear a skeleton.
[Enter LORD MORANZONE all in black; he passes across
the back of the stage looking anxiously about.]

MORANZONE
Where is Guido?
I cannot find him anywhere.

DUCHESS.
[catches sight of him] O God!
'Twas thou who took my love away from me.

MORANZONE
[with a look of joy]
What, has he left you?

DUCHESS.
Nay, you know he has.
Oh, give him back to me, give him back, I say,
Or I will tear your body limb from limb,
And to the common gibbet nail your head
Until the carrion crows have stripped it bare.
Better you had crossed a hungry lioness
Before you came between me and my love.
[With more pathos.]
Nay, give him back, you know not how I love him.
Here by this chair he knelt a half hour since;
'Twas there he stood, and there he looked at me;
This is the hand he kissed, and these the ears
Into whose open portals he did pour
A tale of love so musical that all
The birds stopped singing! Oh, give him back to me.

MORANZONE
He does not love you, Madam.

DUCHESS.
May the plague
Wither the tongue that says so! Give him back.

MORANZONE
Madam, I tell you you will never see him,
Neither to-night, nor any other night.

DUCHESS.
What is your name?

MORANZONE
My name? Revenge!
[Exit.]

DUCHESS.
Revenge!
I think I never harmed a little child.
What should Revenge do coming to my door?
It matters not, for Death is there already,
Waiting with his dim torch to light my way.
'Tis true men hate thee, Death, and yet I think
Thou wilt be kinder to me than my lover,
And so dispatch the messengers at once,
Harry the lazy steeds of lingering day,
And let the night, thy sister, come instead,
And drape the world in mourning; let the owl,
Who is thy minister, scream from his tower
And wake the toad with hooting, and the bat,
That is the slave of dim Persephone,
Wheel through the sombre air on wandering wing!
Tear up the shrieking mandrakes from the earth
And bid them make us music, and tell the mole
To dig deep down thy cold and narrow bed,
For I shall lie within thine arms to-night.

END OF ACT II.

ACT III

SCENE

A large corridor in the Ducal Palace: a window (L.C.) looks out on
a view of Padua by moonlight: a staircase (R.C.) leads up to a
door with a portiere of crimson velvet, with the DUKE's arms

embroidered in gold on it: on the lowest step of the staircase a
figure draped in black is sitting: the hall is lit by an iron
cresset filled with burning tow: thunder and lightning outside:
the time is night.

[Enter GUIDO through the window.]

GUIDO.
The wind is rising: how my ladder shook!
I thought that every gust would break the cords!
[Looks out at the city.]
Christ! What a night:
Great thunder in the heavens, and wild lightnings
Striking from pinnacle to pinnacle
Across the city, till the dim houses seem
To shudder and to shake as each new glare
Dashes adown the street.
[Passes across the stage to foot of staircase.]
Ah! who art thou
That sittest on the stair, like unto Death
Waiting a guilty soul? [A pause.]
Canst thou not speak?
Or has this storm laid palsy on thy tongue,
And chilled thy utterance?
[The figure rises and takes off his mask.]

MORANZONE
Guido Ferranti,
Thy murdered father laughs for joy to-night.

GUIDO.
[confusedly]
What, art thou here?

MORANZONE
Ay, waiting for your coming.

GUIDO.
[looking away from him]
I did not think to see you, but am glad,
That you may know the thing I mean to do.

MORANZONE
First, I would have you know my well-laid plans;
Listen: I have set horses at the gate
Which leads to Parma: when you have done your business
We will ride hence, and by to-morrow night -

GUIDO.
It cannot be.

MORANZONE

Nay, but it shall.

GUIDO.

Listen, Lord MORANZONE,
I am resolved not to kill this man.

MORANZONE

Surely my ears are traitors, speak again:
It cannot be but age has dulled my powers,
I am an old man now: what did you say?
You said that with that dagger in your belt
You would avenge your father's bloody murder;
Did you not say that?

GUIDO.

No, my lord, I said
I was resolved not to kill the DUKE.

MORANZONE

You said not that; it is my senses mock me;
Or else this midnight air o'ercharged with storm
Alters your message in the giving it.

GUIDO.

Nay, you heard rightly; I'll not kill this man.

MORANZONE

What of thine oath, thou traitor, what of thine oath?

GUIDO.

I am resolved not to keep that oath.

MORANZONE

What of thy murdered father?

GUIDO.

Dost thou think
My father would be glad to see me coming,
This old man's blood still hot upon mine hands?

MORANZONE

Ay! he would laugh for joy.

GUIDO.

I do not think so,
There is better knowledge in the other world;
Vengeance is God's, let God himself revenge.

MORANZONE

Thou art God's minister of vengeance.

GUIDO.
No!
God hath no minister but his own hand.
I will not kill this man.

MORANZONE
Why are you here,
If not to kill him, then?

GUIDO.
Lord **MORANZONE** ,
I purpose to ascend to the DUKE's chamber,
And as he lies asleep lay on his breast
The dagger and this writing; when he awakes
Then he will know who held him in his power
And slew him not: this is the noblest vengeance
Which I can take.

MORANZONE
You will not slay him?

GUIDO.
No.

MORANZONE
Ignoble son of a noble father,
Who sufferest this man who sold that father
To live an hour.

GUIDO.
'Twas thou that hindered me;
I would have killed him in the open square,
The day I saw him first.

MORANZONE
It was not yet time;
Now it is time, and, like some green-faced girl,
Thou pratest of forgiveness.

GUIDO.
No! revenge:
The right revenge my father's son should take.

MORANZONE
You are a coward,
Take out the knife, get to the **DUKE** 's chamber,
And bring me back his heart upon the blade.
When he is dead, then you can talk to me
Of noble vengeances.

GUIDO.

Upon thine honour,
And by the love thou bearest my father's name,
Dost thou think my father, that great gentleman,
That generous soldier, that most chivalrous lord,
Would have crept at night-time, like a common thief,
And stabbed an old man sleeping in his bed,
However he had wronged him: tell me that.

MORANZONE

[after some hesitation]
You have sworn an oath, see that you keep that oath.
Boy, do you think I do not know your secret,
Your traffic with the Duchess?

GUIDO.

Silence, liar!
The very moon in heaven is not more chaste.
Nor the white stars so pure.

MORANZONE

And yet, you love her;
Weak fool, to let love in upon your life,
Save as a plaything.

GUIDO.

You do well to talk:
Within your veins, old man, the pulse of youth
Throbs with no ardour. Your eyes full of rheum
Have against Beauty closed their filmy doors,
And your clogged ears, losing their natural sense,
Have shut you from the music of the world.
You talk of love! You know not what it is.

MORANZONE

Oh, in my time, boy, have I walked i' the moon,
Swore I would live on kisses and on blisses,
Swore I would die for love, and did not die,
Wrote love bad verses; ay, and sung them badly,
Like all true lovers: Oh, I have done the tricks!
I know the partings and the chamberings;
We are all animals at best, and love
Is merely passion with a holy name.

GUIDO.

Now then I know you have not loved at all.
Love is the sacrament of life; it sets
Virtue where virtue was not; cleanses men
Of all the vile pollutions of this world;
It is the fire which purges gold from dross,
It is the fan which winnows wheat from chaff,

It is the spring which in some wintry soil
Makes innocence to blossom like a rose.
The days are over when God walked with men,
But Love, which is his image, holds his place.
When a man loves a woman, then he knows
God's secret, and the secret of the world.
There is no house so lowly or so mean,
Which, if their hearts be pure who live in it,
Love will not enter; but if bloody murder
Knock at the Palace gate and is let in,
Love like a wounded thing creeps out and dies.
This is the punishment God sets on sin.
The wicked cannot love.
[A groan comes from the DUKE's chamber.]
Ah! What is that?
Do you not hear? 'Twas nothing.
So I think
That it is woman's mission by their love
To save the souls of men: and loving her,
My Lady, my white Beatrice, I begin
To see a nobler and a holier vengeance
In letting this man live, than doth reside
In bloody deeds o' night, stabs in the dark,
And young hands clutching at a palsied throat.
It was, I think, for love's sake that Lord Christ,
Who was indeed himself incarnate Love,
Bade every man forgive his enemy.

MORANZONE
[sneeringly]
That was in Palestine, not Padua;
And said for saints: I have to do with men.

GUIDO.
It was for all time said.

MORANZONE
And your white Duchess,
What will she do to thank you?

GUIDO.
Alas, I will not see her face again.
'Tis but twelve hours since I parted from her,
So suddenly, and with such violent passion,
That she has shut her heart against me now:
No, I will never see her.

MORANZONE
What will you do?

GUIDO.
After that I have laid the dagger there,
Get hence to-night from Padua.

MORANZONE
And then?

GUIDO.
I will take service with the Doge at Venice,
And bid him pack me straightway to the wars,
And there I will, being now sick of life,
Throw that poor life against some desperate spear.
[A groan from the DUKE's chamber again.]
Did you not hear a voice?

MORANZONE
I always hear,
From the dim confines of some sepulchre,
A voice that cries for vengeance. We waste time,
It will be morning soon; are you resolved
You will not kill the DUKE?

GUIDO.
I am resolved.

MORANZONE
O wretched father, lying unavenged.

GUIDO.
More wretched, were thy son a murderer.

MORANZONE
Why, what is life?

GUIDO.
I do not know, my lord,
I did not give it, and I dare not take it.

MORANZONE
I do not thank God often; but I think
I thank him now that I have got no son!
And you, what bastard blood flows in your veins
That when you have your enemy in your grasp
You let him go! I would that I had left you
With the dull hinds that reared you.

GUIDO.
Better perhaps
That you had done so! May be better still
I'd not been born to this distressful world.

MORANZONE
Farewell!

GUIDO.
Farewell! Some day, Lord MORANZONE,
You will understand my vengeance.

MORANZONE
Never, boy.
[Gets out of window and exit by rope ladder.]

GUIDO.
Father, I think thou knowest my resolve,
And with this nobler vengeance art content.
Father, I think in letting this man live
That I am doing what thou wouldst have done.
Father, I know not if a human voice
Can pierce the iron gateway of the dead,
Or if the dead are set in ignorance
Of what we do, or do not, for their sakes.
And yet I feel a presence in the air,
There is a shadow standing at my side,
And ghostly kisses seem to touch my lips,
And leave them holier. [Kneels down.]
O father, if 'tis thou,
Canst thou not burst through the decrees of death,
And if corporeal semblance show thyself,
That I may touch thy hand!
No, there is nothing. [Rises.]
'Tis the night that cheats us with its phantoms,
And, like a puppet-master, makes us think
That things are real which are not. It grows late.
Now must I to my business.
[Pulls out a letter from his doublet and reads it.]
When he wakes,
And sees this letter, and the dagger with it,
Will he not have some loathing for his life,
Repent, perchance, and lead a better life,
Or will he mock because a young man spared
His natural enemy? I do not care.
Father, it is thy bidding that I do,
Thy bidding, and the bidding of my love
Which teaches me to know thee as thou art.
[Ascends staircase stealthily, and just as he reaches out his hand
to draw back the curtain the Duchess appears all in white. GUIDO
starts back.]

DUCHESS.
Guido! what do you here so late?

GUIDO.
O white and spotless angel of my life,
Sure thou hast come from Heaven with a message
That mercy is more noble than revenge?

DUCHESS.
There is no barrier between us now.

GUIDO.
None, love, nor shall be.

DUCHESS.
I have seen to that.

GUIDO.
Tarry here for me.

DUCHESS.
No, you are not going?
You will not leave me as you did before?

GUIDO.
I will return within a moment's space,
But first I must repair to the DUKE's chamber,
And leave this letter and this dagger there,
That when he wakes -

DUCHESS.
When who wakes?

GUIDO.
Why, the DUKE.

DUCHESS.
He will not wake again.

GUIDO.
What, is he dead?

DUCHESS.
Ay! he is dead.

GUIDO.
O God! how wonderful
Are all thy secret ways! Who would have said
That on this very night, when I had yielded
Into thy hands the vengeance that is thine,
Thou with thy finger wouldst have touched the man,
And bade him come before thy judgment seat.

DUCHESS.
I have just killed him.

GUIDO.
[in horror] Oh!

DUCHESS.
He was asleep;
Come closer, love, and I will tell you all.
I had resolved to kill myself to-night.
About an hour ago I waked from sleep,
And took my dagger from beneath my pillow,
Where I had hidden it to serve my need,
And drew it from the sheath, and felt the edge,
And thought of you, and how I loved you, Guido,
And turned to fall upon it, when I marked
The old man sleeping, full of years and sin;
There lay he muttering curses in his sleep,
And as I looked upon his evil face
Suddenly like a flame there flashed across me,
There is the barrier which Guido spoke of:
You said there lay a barrier between us,
What barrier but he? -
I hardly know
What happened, but a steaming mist of blood
Rose up between us two.

GUIDO.
Oh, horrible!

DUCHESS.
And then he groaned,
And then he groaned no more! I only heard
The dripping of the blood upon the floor.

GUIDO.
Enough, enough.

DUCHESS.
Will you not kiss me now?
Do you remember saying that women's love
Turns men to angels? well, the love of man
Turns women into martyrs; for its sake
We do or suffer anything.

GUIDO.
O God!

DUCHESS.
Will you not speak?

GUIDO.
I cannot speak at all.

DUCHESS.
Let as not talk of this! Let us go hence:
Is not the barrier broken down between us?
What would you more? Come, it is almost morning.
[Puts her hand on GUIDO'S.]

GUIDO.
[breaking from her]
O damned saint! O angel fresh from Hell!
What bloody devil tempted thee to this!
That thou hast killed thy husband, that is nothing -
Hell was already gaping for his soul -
But thou hast murdered Love, and in its place
Hast set a horrible and bloodstained thing,
Whose very breath breeds pestilence and plague,
And strangles Love.

DUCHESS.
[in amazed wonder]
I did it all for you.
I would not have you do it, had you willed it,
For I would keep you without blot or stain,
A thing unblemished, unassailed, untarnished.
Men do not know what women do for love.
Have I not wrecked my soul for your dear sake,
Here and hereafter?

GUIDO.
No, do not touch me,
Between us lies a thin red stream of blood;
I dare not look across it: when you stabbed him
You stabbed Love with a sharp knife to the heart.
We cannot meet again.

DUCHESS.
[wringing her hands]
For you! For you!
I did it all for you: have you forgotten?
You said there was a barrier between us;
That barrier lies now i' the upper chamber
Upset, overthrown, beaten, and battered down,
And will not part us ever.

GUIDO.
No, you mistook:
Sin was the barrier, you have raised it up;
Crime was the barrier, you have set it there.
The barrier was murder, and your hand

Has builded it so high it shuts out heaven,
It shuts out God.

DUCHESS.
I did it all for you;
You dare not leave me now: nay, Guido, listen.
Get horses ready, we will fly to-night.
The past is a bad dream, we will forget it:
Before us lies the future: shall we not have
Sweet days of love beneath our vines and laugh? -
No, no, we will not laugh, but, when we weep,
Well, we will weep together; I will serve you;
I will be very meek and very gentle:
You do not know me.

GUIDO.
Nay, I know you now;
Get hence, I say, out of my sight.

DUCHESS.

[pacing up and down]
O God,
How I have loved this man!

GUIDO.

You never loved me.
Had it been so, Love would have stayed your hand.
How could we sit together at Love's table?
You have poured poison in the sacred wine,
And Murder dips his fingers in the sop.

DUCHESS.
[throws herself on her knees]
Then slay me now! I have spilt blood to-night,
You shall spill more, so we go hand in hand
To heaven or to hell. Draw your sword, Guido.
Quick, let your soul go chambering in my heart,
It will but find its master's image there.
Nay, if you will not slay me with your sword,
Bid me to fall upon this reeking knife,
And I will do it.

GUIDO.
[wresting knife from her]
Give it to me, I say.
O God, your very hands are wet with blood!
This place is Hell, I cannot tarry here.
I pray you let me see your face no more.

DUCHESS.

Better for me I had not seen your face.

[GUIDO recoils: she seizes his hands as she kneels.]

Nay, Guido, listen for a while:

Until you came to Padua I lived

Wretched indeed, but with no murderous thought,

Very submissive to a cruel Lord,

Very obedient to unjust commands,

As pure I think as any gentle girl

Who now would turn in horror from my hands -

[Stands up.]

You came: ah! Guido, the first kindly words

I ever heard since I had come from France

Were from your lips: well, well, that is no matter.

You came, and in the passion of your eyes

I read love's meaning; everything you said

Touched my dumb soul to music, so I loved you.

And yet I did not tell you of my love.

'Twas you who sought me out, knelt at my feet

As I kneel now at yours, and with sweet vows,

[Kneels.]

Whose music seems to linger in my ears,

Swore that you loved me, and I trusted you.

I think there are many women in the world

Who would have tempted you to kill the man.

I did not.

Yet I know that had I done so,

I had not been thus humbled in the dust,

[Stands up.]

But you had loved me very faithfully.

[After a pause approaches him timidly.]

I do not think you understand me, Guido:

It was for your sake that I wrought this deed

Whose horror now chills my young blood to ice,

For your sake only. [Stretching out her arm.]

Will you not speak to me?

Love me a little: in my girlish life

I have been starved for love, and kindliness

Has passed me by.

GUIDO.

I dare not look at you:

You come to me with too pronounced a favour;

Get to your tirewomen.

DUCHESS.

Ay, there it is!

There speaks the man! yet had you come to me

With any heavy sin upon your soul,

Some murder done for hire, not for love,

Why, I had sat and watched at your bedside
All through the night-time, lest Remorse might come
And pour his poisons in your ear, and so
Keep you from sleeping! Sure it is the guilty,
Who, being very wretched, need love most.

GUIDO.
There is no love where there is any guilt.

DUCHESS.
No love where there is any guilt! O God,
How differently do we love from men!
There is many a woman here in Padua,
Some workman's wife, or ruder artisan's,
Whose husband spends the wages of the week
In a coarse revel, or a tavern brawl,
And reeling home late on the Saturday night,
Finds his wife sitting by a fireless hearth,
Trying to hush the child who cries for hunger,
And then sets to and beats his wife because
The child is hungry, and the fire black.
Yet the wife loves him! and will rise next day
With some red bruise across a careworn face,
And sweep the house, and do the common service,
And try and smile, and only be too glad
If he does not beat her a second time
Before her child! that is how women love.
[A pause: GUIDO says nothing.]
I think you will not drive me from your side.
Where have I got to go if you reject me? -
You for whose sake this hand has murdered life,
You for whose sake my soul has wrecked itself
Beyond all hope of pardon.

GUIDO.
Get thee gone:
The dead man is a ghost, and our love too,
Flits like a ghost about its desolate tomb,
And wanders through this charnel house, and weeps
That when you slew your lord you slew it also.
Do you not see?

DUCHESS.
I see when men love women
They give them but a little of their lives,
But women when they love give everything;
I see that, Guido, now.

GUIDO.
Away, away,
And come not back till you have waked your dead.

DUCHESS.

I would to God that I could wake the dead,
Put vision in the glazed eyes, and give
The tongue its natural utterance, and bid
The heart to beat again: that cannot be:
For what is done, is done: and what is dead
Is dead for ever: the fire cannot warm him:
The winter cannot hurt him with its snows;
Something has gone from him; if you call him now,
He will not answer; if you mock him now,
He will not laugh; and if you stab him now
He will not bleed.
I would that I could wake him!
O God, put back the sun a little space,
And from the roll of time blot out to-night,
And bid it not have been! Put back the sun,
And make me what I was an hour ago!
No, no, time will not stop for anything,
Nor the sun stay its courses, though Repentance
Calling it back grow hoarse; but you, my love,
Have you no word of pity even for me?
O Guido, Guido, will you not kiss me once?
Drive me not to some desperate resolve:
Women grow mad when they are treated thus:
Will you not kiss me once?

GUIDO.

[holding up knife]
I will not kiss you
Until the blood grows dry upon this knife,
[Wildly] Back to your dead!

DUCHESS.

[going up the stairs]
Why, then I will be gone! and may you find
More mercy than you showed to me to-night!

GUIDO.

Let me find mercy when I go at night
And do foul murder.

DUCHESS.

[coming down a few steps.]
Murder did you say?
Murder is hungry, and still cries for more,
And Death, his brother, is not satisfied,
But walks the house, and will not go away,
Unless he has a comrade! Tarry, Death,
For I will give thee a most faithful lackey
To travel with thee! Murder, call no more,
For thou shalt eat thy fill.

There is a storm
Will break upon this house before the morning,
So horrible, that the white moon already
Turns grey and sick with terror, the low wind
Goes moaning round the house, and the high stars
Run madly through the vaulted firmament,
As though the night wept tears of liquid fire
For what the day shall look upon. Oh, weep,
Thou lamentable heaven! Weep thy fill!
Though sorrow like a cataract drench the fields,
And make the earth one bitter lake of tears,
It would not be enough. [A peal of thunder.]
Do you not hear,
There is artillery in the Heaven to-night.
Vengeance is wakened up, and has unloosed
His dogs upon the world, and in this matter
Which lies between us two, let him who draws
The thunder on his head beware the ruin
Which the forked flame brings after.
[A flash of lightning followed by a peal of thunder.]

GUIDO.
Away! away!
[Exit the DUCHESS, who as she lifts the crimson curtain looks back
for a moment at GUIDO, but he makes no sign. More thunder.]
Now is life fallen in ashes at my feet
And noble love self-slain; and in its place
Crept murder with its silent bloody feet.
And she who wrought it, Oh! and yet she loved me,
And for my sake did do this dreadful thing.
I have been cruel to her: Beatrice!
Beatrice, I say, come back.
[Begins to ascend staircase, when the noise of Soldiers is heard.]
Ah! what is that?
Torches ablaze, and noise of hurrying feet.
Pray God they have not seized her.
[Noise grows louder.]
Beatrice!
There is yet time to escape. Come down, come out!
[The voice of the DUCHESS outside.]
This way went he, the man who slew my lord.
[Down the staircase comes hurrying a confused body of Soldiers;
GUIDO is not seen at first, till the DUCHESS surrounded by SERVANTs
carrying torches appears at the top of the staircase, and points to
GUIDO, who is seized at once, one of the Soldiers dragging the
knife from his hand and showing it to the Captain of the Guard in
sight of the audience. Tableau.]

END OF ACT III.

ACT IV

SCENE

The Court of Justice: the walls are hung with stamped grey velvet:
above the hangings the wall is red, and gilt symbolical figures
bear up the roof, which is made of red beams with grey soffits and
moulding: a canopy of white satin flowered with gold is set for
the Duchess: below it a long bench with red cloth for the Judges:
below that a table for the clerks of the court. Two soldiers stand
on each side of the canopy, and two soldiers guard the door; the
citizens have some of them collected in the Court; others are
coming in greeting one another; two TIPSTAFFs in violet keep order
with long white wands.

FIRST CITIZEN
Good morrow, neighbour Anthony.

SECOND CITIZEN
Good morrow, neighbour Dominick.

FIRST CITIZEN
This is a strange day for Padua, is it not? the DUKE being dead.

SECOND CITIZEN
I tell you, neighbour Dominick, I have not known such a day since
the last DUKE died.

FIRST CITIZEN
They will try him first, and sentence him afterwards, will they
not, neighbour Anthony?

SECOND CITIZEN
Nay, for he might 'scape his punishment then; but they will condemn
him first so that he gets his deserts, and give him trial
afterwards so that no injustice is done.

FIRST CITIZEN
Well, well, it will go hard with him I doubt not.

SECOND CITIZEN
Surely it is a grievous thing to shed a DUKE's blood.

THIRD CITIZEN
They say a DUKE has blue blood.

SECOND CITIZEN
I think our **DUKE** 's blood was black like his soul.

FIRST CITIZEN
Have a watch, neighbour Anthony, the officer is looking at thee.

SECOND CITIZEN
I care not if he does but look at me; he cannot whip me with the lashes of his eye.

THIRD CITIZEN
What think you of this young man who stuck the knife into the DUKE?

SECOND CITIZEN
Why, that he is a well-behaved, and a well-meaning, and a well-favoured lad, and yet wicked in that he killed the DUKE.

THIRD CITIZEN
'Twas the first time he did it: may be the law will not be hard on him, as he did not do it before.

SECOND CITIZEN
True.

TIPSTAFF
Silence, knave.

SECOND CITIZEN
Am I thy looking-glass, Master TIPSTAFF, that thou callest me knave?

FIRST CITIZEN
Here be one of the household coming. Well, Dame Lucy, thou art of the Court, how does thy poor mistress the Duchess, with her sweet face?

MISTRESS LUCY
O well-a-day! O miserable day! O day! O misery! Why it is just nineteen years last June, at Michaelmas, since I was married to my husband, and it is August now, and here is the DUKE murdered; there is a coincidence for you!

SECOND CITIZEN
Why, if it is a coincidence, they may not kill the young man: there is no law against coincidences.

FIRST CITIZEN
But how does the Duchess?

MISTRESS LUCY
Well well, I knew some harm would happen to the house: six weeks ago the cakes were all burned on one side, and last Saint Martin even as ever was, there flew into the candle a big moth that had wings, and a'most scared me.

FIRST CITIZEN
But come to the Duchess, good gossip: what of her?

MISTRESS LUCY
Marry, it is time you should ask after her, poor lady; she is
distraught almost. Why, she has not slept, but paced the chamber
all night long. I prayed her to have a posset, or some aqua-vitae,
and to get to bed and sleep a little for her health's sake, but she
answered me she was afraid she might dream. That was a strange
answer, was it not?

SECOND CITIZEN
These great folk have not much sense, so Providence makes it up to
them in fine clothes.

MISTRESS LUCY
Well, well, God keep murder from us, I say, as long as we are
alive.

[Enter LORD MORANZONE hurriedly.]

MORANZONE
Is the DUKE dead?

SECOND CITIZEN
He has a knife in his heart, which they say is not healthy for any
man.

MORANZONE
Who is accused of having killed him?

SECOND CITIZEN
Why, the prisoner, sir.

MORANZONE
But who is the prisoner?

SECOND CITIZEN
Why, he that is accused of the DUKE's murder.

MORANZONE
I mean, what is his name?

SECOND CITIZEN
Faith, the same which his godfathers gave him: what else should it
be?

TIPSTAFF
Guido Ferranti is his name, my lord.

MORANZONE

I almost knew thine answer ere you gave it.
[Aside.]
Yet it is strange he should have killed the DUKE,
Seeing he left me in such different mood.
It is most likely when he saw the man,
This devil who had sold his father's life,
That passion from their seat within his heart
Thrust all his boyish theories of love,
And in their place set vengeance; yet I marvel
That he escaped not.
[Turning again to the crowd.]
How was he taken? Tell me.

THIRD CITIZEN

Marry, sir, he was taken by the heels.

MORANZONE

But who seized him?

THIRD CITIZEN

Why, those that did lay hold of him.

MORANZONE

How was the alarm given?

THIRD CITIZEN

That I cannot tell you, sir.

MISTRESS LUCY

It was the Duchess herself who pointed him out.

MORANZONE

[aside]
The Duchess! There is something strange in this.

MISTRESS LUCY

Ay! And the dagger was in his hand, the Duchess's own dagger.

MORANZONE

What did you say?

MISTRESS LUCY

Why, marry, that it was with the Duchess's dagger that the DUKE was killed.

MORANZONE

[aside]
There is some mystery about this: I cannot understand it.

SECOND CITIZEN
They be very long a-coming,

FIRST CITIZEN
I warrant they will come soon enough for the prisoner.

TIPSTAFF
Silence in the Court!

FIRST CITIZEN
Thou dost break silence in bidding us keep it, Master TIPSTAFF.
[Enter the LORD JUSTICE and the other Judges.]

SECOND CITIZEN
Who is he in scarlet? Is he the HEADSMAN?

THIRD CITIZEN
Nay, he is the LORD JUSTICE.
[Enter GUIDO guarded.]

SECOND CITIZEN
There be the prisoner surely.

THIRD CITIZEN
He looks honest.

FIRST CITIZEN
That be his villany: knaves nowadays do look so honest that honest
folk are forced to look like knaves so as to be different.
[Enter the Headman, who takes his stand behind GUIDO.]

SECOND CITIZEN
Yon be the HEADSMAN then! O Lord! Is the axe sharp, think you?

FIRST CITIZEN
Ay! sharper than thy wits are; but the edge is not towards him,
mark you.

SECOND CITIZEN
[scratching his neck]
I' faith, I like it not so near.

FIRST CITIZEN
Tut, thou need'st not be afraid; they never cut the heads of common
folk: they do but hang us.
[Trumpets outside.]

THIRD CITIZEN
What are the trumpets for? Is the trial over?

FIRST CITIZEN
Nay, 'tis for the Duchess.
[Enter the DUCHESS in black velvet; her train of flowered black
velvet is carried by two pages in violet; with her is the **CARDINAL**
in scarlet, and the gentlemen of the Court in black; she takes her
seat on the throne above the Judges, who rise and take their caps
off as she enters; the CARDINAL sits next to her a little lower;
the Courtiers group themselves about the throne.]

SECOND CITIZEN
O poor lady, how pale she is! Will she sit there?

FIRST CITIZEN
Ay! she is in the DUKE's place now.

SECOND CITIZEN
That is a good thing for Padua; the Duchess is a very kind and
merciful Duchess; why, she cured my child of the ague once.

THIRD CITIZEN
Ay, and has given us bread: do not forget the bread.

A SOLDIER
Stand back, good people.

SECOND CITIZEN
If we be good, why should we stand back?

TIPSTAFF
Silence in the Court!

LORD JUSTICE
May it please your Grace,
Is it your pleasure we proceed to trial
Of the DUKE's murder? [DUCHESS bows.]
Set the prisoner forth.
What is thy name?

GUIDO.
It matters not, my lord.

LORD JUSTICE
Guido Ferranti is thy name in Padua.

GUIDO.
A man may die as well under that name as any other.

LORD JUSTICE
Thou art not ignorant
What dreadful charge men lay against thee here,
Namely, the treacherous murder of thy Lord,

Simone Gesso, DUKE of Padua;
What dost thou say in answer?

GUIDO.
I say nothing.

LORD JUSTICE
[rising]
Guido Ferranti -

MORANZONE
[stepping from the crowd]
Tarry, my LORD JUSTICE.

LORD JUSTICE
Who art thou that bid'st justice tarry, sir?

MORANZONE
So be it justice it can go its way;
But if it be not justice -

LORD JUSTICE
Who is this?

COUNT BARDI
A very noble gentleman, and well known
To the late DUKE.

LORD JUSTICE
Sir, thou art come in time
To see the murder of the DUKE avenged.
There stands the man who did this heinous thing.

MORANZONE
My lord,
I ask again what proof have ye?

LORD JUSTICE
[holding up the dagger]
This dagger,
Which from his blood-stained hands, itself all blood,
Last night the soldiers seized: what further proof
Need we indeed?

MORANZONE
[takes the danger and approaches the DUCHESS]
Saw I not such a dagger
Hang from your Grace's girdle yesterday?
[The DUCHESS shudders and makes no answer.]
Ah! my LORD JUSTICE, may I speak a moment
With this young man, who in such peril stands?

LORD JUSTICE

Ay, willingly, my lord, and may you turn him
To make a full avowal of his guilt.
[LORD MORANZONE goes over to GUIDO, who stands R. and clutches him
by the hand.]

MORANZONE

[in a low voice]
She did it! Nay, I saw it in her eyes.
Boy, dost thou think I'll let thy father's son
Be by this woman butchered to his death?
Her husband sold your father, and the wife
Would sell the son in turn.

GUIDO.

Lord MORANZONE,
I alone did this thing: be satisfied,
My father is avenged.

LORD JUSTICE

Doth he confess?

GUIDO.

My lord, I do confess
That foul unnatural murder has been done.

FIRST CITIZEN

Why, look at that: he has a pitiful heart, and does not like
murder; they will let him go for that.

LORD JUSTICE

Say you no more?

GUIDO.

My lord, I say this also,
That to spill human blood is deadly sin.

SECOND CITIZEN

Marry, he should tell that to the HEADSMAN: 'tis a good sentiment.

GUIDO.

Lastly, my lord, I do entreat the Court
To give me leave to utter openly
The dreadful secret of this mystery,
And to point out the very guilty one
Who with this dagger last night slew the DUKE.

LORD JUSTICE

Thou hast leave to speak.

DUCHESS.
[rising]
I say he shall not speak:
What need have we of further evidence?
Was he not taken in the house at night
In Guilt's own bloody livery?

LORD JUSTICE
[showing her the statute]
Your Grace
Can read the law.

DUCHESS.
[waiving book aside]
Bethink you, my LORD JUSTICE,
Is it not very like that such a one
May, in the presence of the people here,
Utter some slanderous word against my Lord,
Against the city, or the city's honour,
Perchance against myself.

LORD JUSTICE
My liege, the law.

DUCHESS.
He shall not speak, but, with gags in his mouth,
Shall climb the ladder to the bloody block.

LORD JUSTICE
The law, my liege.

DUCHESS.
We are not bound by law,
But with it we bind others.

MORANZONE
My LORD JUSTICE,
Thou wilt not suffer this injustice here.

LORD JUSTICE
The Court needs not thy voice, Lord MORANZONE.
Madam, it were a precedent most evil
To wrest the law from its appointed course,
For, though the cause be just, yet anarchy
Might on this licence touch these golden scales
And unjust causes unjust victories gain.

COUNT BARDI
I do not think your Grace can stay the law.

DUCHESS.
Ay, it is well to preach and prate of law:
Methinks, my haughty lords of Padua,
If ye are hurt in pocket or estate,
So much as makes your monstrous revenues
Less by the value of one ferry toll,
Ye do not wait the tedious law's delay
With such sweet patience as ye counsel me.

COUNT BARDI
Madam, I think you wrong our nobles here.

DUCHESS.
I think I wrong them not. Which of you all
Finding a thief within his house at night,
With some poor chattel thrust into his rags,
Will stop and parley with him? do ye not
Give him unto the officer and his hook
To be dragged gaolwards straightway?
And so now,
Had ye been men, finding this fellow here,
With my Lord's life still hot upon his hands,
Ye would have haled him out into the court,
And struck his head off with an axe.

GUIDO.
O God!

DUCHESS.
Speak, my LORD JUSTICE.

LORD JUSTICE
Your Grace, it cannot be:
The laws of Padua are most certain here:
And by those laws the common murderer even
May with his own lips plead, and make defence.

DUCHESS.
This is no common murderer,LORD JUSTICE,
But a great outlaw, and a most vile traitor,
Taken in open arms against the state.
For he who slays the man who rules a state
Slays the state also, widows every wife,
And makes each child an orphan, and no less
Is to be held a public enemy,
Than if he came with mighty ordonnance,
And all the spears of Venice at his back,
To beat and batter at our city gates -
Nay, is more dangerous to our commonwealth,
For walls and gates, bastions and forts, and things
Whose common elements are wood and stone

May be raised up, but who can raise again
The ruined body of my murdered lord,
And bid it live and laugh?

MAFFIO
Now by Saint Paul
I do not think that they will let him speak.

JEPPO VITELLOZZO
There is much in this, listen.

DUCHESS.
Wherefore now,
Throw ashes on the head of Padua,
With sable banners hang each silent street,
Let every man be clad in solemn black;
But ere we turn to these sad rites of mourning
Let us bethink us of the desperate hand
Which wrought and brought this ruin on our state,
And straightway pack him to that narrow house,
Where no voice is, but with a little dust
Death fills right up the lying mouths of men.

GUIDO.
Unhand me, knaves! I tell thee, my LORD JUSTICE,
Thou mightst as well bid the untrammelled ocean,
The winter whirlwind, or the Alpine storm,
Not roar their will, as bid me hold my peace!
Ay! though ye put your knives into my throat,
Each grim and gaping wound shall find a tongue,
And cry against you.

LORD JUSTICE
Sir, this violence
Avails you nothing; for save the tribunal
Give thee a lawful right to open speech,
Naught that thou sayest can be credited.
[The DUCHESS smiles and GUIDO falls back with a gesture of
despair.]
Madam, myself, and these wise Justices,
Will with your Grace's sanction now retire
Into another chamber, to decide
Upon this difficult matter of the law,
And search the statutes and the precedents.

DUCHESS.
Go, my LORD JUSTICE, search the statutes well,
Nor let this brawling traitor have his way.

MORANZONE
Go, my LORD JUSTICE, search thy conscience well,

Nor let a man be sent to death unheard.
[Exit the LORD JUSTICE and the Judges.]

DUCHESS.
Silence, thou evil genius of my life!
Thou com'st between us two a second time;
This time, my lord, I think the turn is mine.

GUIDO.
I shall not die till I have uttered voice.

DUCHESS.
Thou shalt die silent, and thy secret with thee.

GUIDO.
Art thou that Beatrice, Duchess of Padua?

DUCHESS.
I am what thou hast made me; look at me well,
I am thy handiwork.

MAFFIO
See, is she not
Like that white tigress which we saw at Venice,
Sent by some Indian soldan to the Doge?

JEPPO
Hush! she may hear thy chatter.

HEADSMAN
My young fellow,
I do not know why thou shouldst care to speak,
Seeing my axe is close upon thy neck,
And words of thine will never blunt its edge.
But if thou art so bent upon it, why
Thou mightest plead unto the Churchman yonder:
The common people call him kindly here,
Indeed I know he has a kindly soul.

GUIDO.
This man, whose trade is death, hath courtesies
More than the others.

HEADSMAN
Why, God love you, sir,
I'll do you your last service on this earth.

GUIDO.
My good Lord CARDINAL, in a Christian land,
With Lord Christ's face of mercy looking down
From the high seat of Judgment, shall a man

Die unabsolved, unshrived? And if not so,
May I not tell this dreadful tale of sin,
If any sin there be upon my soul?

DUCHESS.
Thou dost but waste thy time.

CARDINAL
Alack, my son,
I have no power with the secular arm.
My task begins when justice has been done,
To urge the wavering sinner to repent
And to confess to Holy Church's ear
The dreadful secrets of a sinful mind.

DUCHESS.
Thou mayest speak to the confessional
Until thy lips grow weary of their tale,
But here thou shalt not speak.

GUIDO.
My reverend father,
You bring me but cold comfort.

CARDINAL
Nay, my son,
For the great power of our mother Church,
Ends not with this poor bubble of a world,
Of which we are but dust, as Jerome saith,
For if the sinner doth repentant die,
Our prayers and holy masses much avail
To bring the guilty soul from purgatory.

DUCHESS.
And when in purgatory thou seest my Lord
With that red star of blood upon his heart,
Tell him I sent thee hither.

GUIDO.
O dear God!

MORANZONE
This is the woman, is it, whom you loved?

CARDINAL
Your Grace is very cruel to this man.

DUCHESS.
No more than he was cruel to her Grace.

CARDINAL
Yet mercy is the sovereign right of princes.

DUCHESS.
I got no mercy, and I give it not.
He hath changed my heart into a heart of stone,
He hath sown rank nettles in a goodly field,
He hath poisoned the wells of pity in my breast,
He hath withered up all kindness at the root;
My life is as some famine murdered land,
Whence all good things have perished utterly:
I am what he hath made me.
[The DUCHESS weeps.]

JEPPO
Is it not strange
That she should so have loved the wicked DUKE?

MAFFIO
It is most strange when women love their lords,
And when they love them not it is most strange.

JEPPO
What a philosopher thou art, Petrucci!

MAFFIO
Ay! I can bear the ills of other men,
Which is philosophy.

DUCHESS.
They tarry long,
These greybeards and their council; bid them come;
Bid them come quickly, else I think my heart
Will beat itself to bursting: not indeed,
That I here care to live; God knows my life
Is not so full of joy, yet, for all that,
I would not die companionless, or go
Lonely to Hell.
Look, my Lord CARDINAL,
Canst thou not see across my forehead here,
In scarlet letters writ, the word Revenge?
Fetch me some water, I will wash it off:
'Twas branded there last night, but in the day-time
I need not wear it, need I, my Lord CARDINAL?
Oh, how it sears and burns into my brain:
Give me a knife; not that one, but another,
And I will cut it out.

CARDINAL
It is most natural

To be incensed against the murderous hand
That treacherously stabbed your sleeping lord.

DUCHESS.
I would, old CARDINAL, I could burn that hand;
But it will burn hereafter.

CARDINAL
Nay, the Church
Ordains us to forgive our enemies.

DUCHESS.
Forgiveness? what is that? I never got it.
They come at last: well, my LORD JUSTICE, well.
[Enter the LORD JUSTICE.]

LORD JUSTICE
Most gracious Lady, and our sovereign Liege,
We have long pondered on the point at issue,
And much considered of your Grace's wisdom,
And never wisdom spake from fairer lips -

DUCHESS.
Proceed, sir, without compliment.

LORD JUSTICE
We find,
As your own Grace did rightly signify,
That any citizen, who by force or craft
Conspires against the person of the Liege,
Is ipso facto outlaw, void of rights
Such as pertain to other citizens,
Is traitor, and a public enemy,
Who may by any casual sword be slain
Without the slayer's danger; nay, if brought
Into the presence of the tribunal,
Must with dumb lips and silence reverent
Listen unto his well-deserved doom,
Nor has the privilege of open speech.

DUCHESS.
I thank thee, my LORD JUSTICE, heartily;
I like your law: and now I pray dispatch
This public outlaw to his righteous doom;
What is there more?

LORD JUSTICE
Ay, there is more, your Grace.
This man being alien born, not Paduan,
Nor by allegiance bound unto the DUKE,
Save such as common nature doth lay down,

Hath, though accused of treasons manifold,
Whose slightest penalty is certain death,
Yet still the right of public utterance
Before the people and the open court;
Nay, shall be much entreated by the Court,
To make some formal pleading for his life,
Lest his own city, righteously incensed,
Should with an unjust trial tax our state,
And wars spring up against the commonwealth:
So merciful are the laws of Padua
Unto the stranger living in her gates.

DUCHESS.
Being of my Lord's household, is he stranger here?

LORD JUSTICE
Ay, until seven years of service spent
He cannot be a Paduan citizen.

GUIDO.
I thank thee, my LORD JUSTICE, heartily;
I like your law.

SECOND CITIZEN
I like no law at all:
Were there no law there'd be no law-breakers,
So all men would be virtuous.

FIRST CITIZEN
So they would;
'Tis a wise saying that, and brings you far.

TIPSTAFF
Ay! to the gallows, knave.

DUCHESS.
Is this the law?

LORD JUSTICE
It is the law most certainly, my liege.

DUCHESS.
Show me the book: 'tis written in blood-red.

JEPPO
Look at the Duchess.

DUCHESS.
Thou accursed law,
I would that I could tear thee from the state
As easy as I tear thee from this book.

[Tears out the page.]
Come here, COUNT BARDI: are you honourable?
Get a horse ready for me at my house,
For I must ride to Venice instantly.

COUNT BARDI
To Venice, Madam?

DUCHESS.
Not a word of this,
Go, go at once. [Exit COUNT BARDI.]
A moment, my LORD JUSTICE.
If, as thou sayest it, this is the law -
Nay, nay, I doubt not that thou sayest right,
Though right be wrong in such a case as this -
May I not by the virtue of mine office
Adjourn this court until another day?

LORD JUSTICE
Madam, you cannot stay a trial for blood.

DUCHESS.
I will not tarry then to hear this man
Rail with rude tongue against our sacred person.
Come, gentlemen.

LORD JUSTICE
My liege,
You cannot leave this court until the prisoner
Be purged or guilty of this dread offence.

DUCHESS.
Cannot, LORD JUSTICE? By what right do you
Set barriers in my path where I should go?
Am I not Duchess here in Padua,
And the state's regent?

LORD JUSTICE
For that reason, Madam,
Being the fountain-head of life and death
Whence, like a mighty river, justice flows,
Without thy presence justice is dried up
And fails of purpose: thou must tarry here.

DUCHESS.
What, wilt thou keep me here against my will?

LORD JUSTICE
We pray thy will be not against the law.

DUCHESS.
What if I force my way out of the court?

LORD JUSTICE
Thou canst not force the Court to give thee way.

DUCHESS.
I will not tarry. [Rises from her seat.]

LORD JUSTICE
Is the USHER here?
Let him stand forth. [USHER comes forward.]
Thou knowest thy business, sir.
[The USHER closes the doors of the court, which are L., and when
the DUCHESS and her retinue approach, kneels down.]

USHER
In all humility I beseech your Grace
Turn not my duty to discourtesy,
Nor make my unwelcome office an offence.

DUCHESS.
Is there no gentleman amongst you all
To prick this prating fellow from our way?

MAFFIO
[drawing his sword]
Ay! that will I.

LORD JUSTICE
Count MAFFIO, have a care,
And you, sir. [To JEPPO.]
The first man who draws his sword
Upon the meanest officer of this Court,
Dies before nightfall.

DUCHESS.
Sirs, put up your swords:
It is most meet that I should hear this man.
[Goes back to throne.]

MORANZONE
Now hast thou got thy enemy in thy hand.

LORD JUSTICE
[taking the time-glass up]
Guido Ferranti, while the crumbling sand
Falls through this time-glass, thou hast leave to speak.
This and no more.

GUIDO.
It is enough, my lord.

LORD JUSTICE
Thou standest on the extreme verge of death;
See that thou speakest nothing but the truth,
Naught else will serve thee.

GUIDO.
If I speak it not,
Then give my body to the HEADSMAN there.

LORD JUSTICE
[turns the time-glass]
Let there be silence while the prisoner speaks.

TIPSTAFF
Silence in the Court there.

GUIDO.
My Lords Justices,
And reverent judges of this worthy court,
I hardly know where to begin my tale,
So strangely dreadful is this history.
First, let me tell you of what birth I am.
I am the son of that good DUKE Lorenzo
Who was with damned treachery done to death
By a most wicked villain, lately DUKE
Of this good town of Padua.

LORD JUSTICE
Have a care,
It will avail thee nought to mock this prince
Who now lies in his coffin.

MAFFIO
By Saint James,
This is the DUKE of Parma's rightful heir.

JEPPO
I always thought him noble.

GUIDO.
I confess
That with the purport of a just revenge,
A most just vengeance on a man of blood,
I entered the DUKE's household, served his will,
Sat at his board, drank of his wine, and was
His intimate: so much I will confess,
And this too, that I waited till he grew
To give the fondest secrets of his life

Into my keeping, till he fawned on me,
And trusted me in every private matter
Even as my noble father trusted him;
That for this thing I waited.
[To the HEADSMAN.] Thou man of blood!
Turn not thine axe on me before the time:
Who knows if it be time for me to die?
Is there no other neck in court but mine?

LORD JUSTICE
The sand within the time-glass flows apace.
Come quickly to the murder of the DUKE.

GUIDO.
I will be brief: Last night at twelve o' the clock,
By a strong rope I scaled the palace wall,
With purport to revenge my father's murder -
Ay! with that purport I confess, my lord.
This much I will acknowledge, and this also,
That as with stealthy feet I climbed the stair
Which led unto the chamber of the DUKE,
And reached my hand out for the scarlet cloth
Which shook and shivered in the gusty door,
Lo! the white moon that sailed in the great heaven
Flooded with silver light the darkened room,
Night lit her candles for me, and I saw
The man I hated, cursing in his sleep;
And thinking of a most dear father murdered,
Sold to the scaffold, bartered to the block,
I smote the treacherous villain to the heart
With this same dagger, which by chance I found
Within the chamber.

DUCHESS.
[rising from her seat]
Oh!

GUIDO.
[hurriedly]
I killed the DUKE.
Now, my LORD JUSTICE, if I may crave a boon,
Suffer me not to see another sun
Light up the misery of this loathsome world.

LORD JUSTICE
Thy boon is granted, thou shalt die to-night.
Lead him away. Come, Madam
[GUIDO is led off; as he goes the DUCHESS stretches out her arms
and rushes down the stage.]

DUCHESS.
Guido! Guido!
[Faints.]

Tableau

END OF ACT IV.

ACT V

SCENE

A dungeon in the public prison of Padua; Guido lies asleep on a
pallet (L.C.); a table with a goblet on it is set (L.C.); five
soldiers are drinking and playing dice in the corner on a stone
table; one of them has a lantern hung to his halbert; a torch is
set in the wall over Guido's head. Two grated windows behind, one
on each side of the door which is (C.), look out into the passage;
the stage is rather dark.

FIRST SOLDIER
[throws dice]
Sixes again! good Pietro.

SECOND SOLDIER
I' faith, lieutenant, I will play with thee no more. I will lose
everything.

THIRD SOLDIER
Except thy wits; thou art safe there!

SECOND SOLDIER
Ay, ay, he cannot take them from me.

THIRD SOLDIER
No; for thou hast no wits to give him.

THE SOLDIERS
[loudly]
Ha! ha! ha!

FIRST SOLDIER
Silence! You will wake the prisoner; he is asleep.

SECOND SOLDIER
What matter? He will get sleep enough when he is buried. I
warrant he'd be glad if we could wake him when he's in the grave.

THIRD SOLDIER

Nay! for when he wakes there it will be judgment day.

SECOND SOLDIER

Ay, and he has done a grievous thing; for, look you, to murder one of us who are but flesh and blood is a sin, and to kill a DUKE goes being near against the law.

FIRST SOLDIER

Well, well, he was a wicked DUKE.

SECOND SOLDIER

And so he should not have touched him; if one meddles with wicked people, one is like to be tainted with their wickedness.

THIRD SOLDIER

Ay, that is true. How old is the prisoner?

SECOND SOLDIER

Old enough to do wrong, and not old enough to be wise.

FIRST SOLDIER

Why, then, he might be any age.

SECOND SOLDIER

They say the Duchess wanted to pardon him.

FIRST SOLDIER

Is that so?

SECOND SOLDIER

Ay, and did much entreat the LORD JUSTICE, but he would not.

FIRST SOLDIER

I had thought, Pietro, that the Duchess was omnipotent.

SECOND SOLDIER

True, she is well-favoured; I know none so comely.

THE SOLDIERS

Ha! ha! ha!

FIRST SOLDIER

I meant I had thought our Duchess could do anything.

SECOND SOLDIER

Nay, for he is now given over to the Justices, and they will see that justice be done; they and stout Hugh the HEADSMAN; but when his head is off, why then the Duchess can pardon him if she likes; there is no law against that.

FIRST SOLDIER
I do not think that stout Hugh, as you call him, will do the
business for him after all. This Guido is of gentle birth, and so
by the law can drink poison first, if it so be his pleasure.

THIRD SOLDIER
And if he does not drink it?

FIRST SOLDIER
Why, then, they will kill him.
[Knocking comes at the door.]

FIRST SOLDIER
See who that is.
[**THIRD SOLDIER** goes over and looks through the wicket.]

THIRD SOLDIER
It is a woman, sir.

FIRST SOLDIER
Is she pretty?

THIRD SOLDIER
I can't tell. She is masked, lieutenant.

FIRST SOLDIER
It is only very ugly or very beautiful women who ever hide their
faces. Let her in.
[Soldier opens the door, and the DUCHESS masked and cloaked
enters.]

DUCHESS.
[to Third Soldier]
Are you the officer on guard?

FIRST SOLDIER
[coming forward]
I am, madam.

DUCHESS.
I must see the prisoner alone.

FIRST SOLDIER
I am afraid that is impossible. [The DUCHESS hands him a ring, he
looks at and returns it to her with a bow and makes a sign to the
Soldiers.] Stand without there. [Exeunt the Soldiers.]

DUCHESS.
Officer, your men are somewhat rough.

FIRST SOLDIER
They mean no harm.

DUCHESS.
I shall be going back in a few minutes. As I pass through the
corridor do not let them try and lift my mask.

FIRST SOLDIER
You need not be afraid, madam.

DUCHESS.
I have a particular reason for wishing my face not to be seen.

FIRST SOLDIER
Madam, with this ring you can go in and out as you please; it is
the Duchess's own ring.

DUCHESS.
Leave us. [The Soldier turns to go out.] A moment, sir. For what
hour is . . .

FIRST SOLDIER
At twelve o'clock, madam, we have orders to lead him out; but I
dare say he won't wait for us; he's more like to take a drink out
of that poison yonder. Men are afraid of the HEADSMAN.

DUCHESS.
Is that poison?

FIRST SOLDIER
Ay, madam, and very sure poison too.

DUCHESS.
You may go, sir.

FIRST SOLDIER
By Saint James, a pretty hand! I wonder who she is. Some woman
who loved him, perhaps. [Exit.]

DUCHESS.
[taking her mark off] At last!
He can escape now in this cloak and vizard,
We are of a height almost: they will not know him;
As for myself what matter?
So that he does not curse me as he goes,
I care but little: I wonder will he curse me.
He has the right. It is eleven now;
They will not come till twelve.
[Goes over to the table.]
So this is poison.
Is it not strange that in this liquor here

There lies the key to all philosophies?
[Takes the cup up.]
It smells of poppies. I remember well
That, when I was a child in Sicily,
I took the scarlet poppies from the corn,
And made a little wreath, and my grave uncle,
Don John of Naples, laughed: I did not know
That they had power to stay the springs of life,
To make the pulse cease beating, and to chill
The blood in its own vessels, till men come
And with a hook hale the poor body out,
And throw it in a ditch: the body, ay, -
What of the soul? that goes to heaven or hell.
Where will mine go?
[Takes the torch from the wall, and goes over to the bed.]
How peacefully here he sleeps,
Like a young schoolboy tired out with play:
I would that I could sleep so peacefully,
But I have dreams. [Bending over him.]
Poor boy: what if I kissed him?
No, no, my lips would burn him like a fire.
He has had enough of Love. Still that white neck
Will 'scape the HEADSMAN: I have seen to that:
He will get hence from Padua to-night,
And that is well. You are very wise, LORD JUSTICE,
And yet you are not half so wise as I am,
And that is well.
O God! how I have loved you,
And what a bloody flower did Love bear!
[Comes back to the table.]
What if I drank these juices, and so ceased?
Were it not better than to wait till Death
Come to my bed with all his serving men,
Remorse, disease, old age, and misery?
I wonder does one suffer much: I think
That I am very young to die like this,
But so it must be. Why, why should I die?
He will escape to-night, and so his blood
Will not be on my head. No, I must die;
I have been guilty, therefore I must die;
He loves me not, and therefore I must die:
I would die happier if he would kiss me,
But he will not do that. I did not know him.
I thought he meant to sell me to the Judge;
That is not strange; we women never know
Our lovers till they leave us.
[Bell begins to toll]
Thou vile bell,
That like a bloodhound from thy brazen throat
Call'st for this man's life, cease! thou shalt not get it.
He stirs, I must be quick: [Takes up cup.]

O Love, Love, Love,
I did not think that I would pledge thee thus!
[Drinks poison, and sets the cup down on the table behind her: the
noise wakens GUIDO, who starts up, and does not see what she has
done. There is silence for a minute, each looking at the other.]
I do not come to ask your pardon now,
Seeing I know I stand beyond all pardon;
Enough of that: I have already, sir,
Confessed my sin to the Lords Justices;
They would not listen to me: and some said
I did invent a tale to save your life;
You have trafficked with me; others said
That women played with pity as with men;
Others that grief for my slain Lord and husband
Had robbed me of my wits: they would not hear me,
And, when I sware it on the holy book,
They bade the doctor cure me. They are ten,
Ten against one, and they possess your life.
They call me Duchess here in Padua.
I do not know, sir; if I be the Duchess,
I wrote your pardon, and they would not take it;
They call it treason, say I taught them that;
Maybe I did. Within an hour, Guido,
They will be here, and drag you from the cell,
And bind your hands behind your back, and bid you
Kneel at the block: I am before them there;
Here is the signet ring of Padua,
'Twill bring you safely through the men on guard;
There is my cloak and vizard; they have orders
Not to be curious: when you pass the gate
Turn to the left, and at the second bridge
You will find horses waiting: by to-morrow
You will be at Venice, safe. [A pause.]
Do you not speak?
Will you not even curse me ere you go? -
You have the right. [A pause.]
You do not understand
There lies between you and the HEADSMAN's axe
Hardly so much sand in the hour-glass
As a child's palm could carry: here is the ring:
I have washed my hand: there is no blood upon it:
You need not fear. Will you not take the ring?

GUIDO.
[takes ring and kisses it]
Ay! gladly, Madam.

DUCHESS.
And leave Padua.

GUIDO.
Leave Padua.

DUCHESS.
But it must be to-night.

GUIDO.
To-night it shall be.

DUCHESS.
Oh, thank God for that!

GUIDO.
So I can live; life never seemed so sweet
As at this moment.

DUCHESS.
Do not tarry, Guido,
There is my cloak: the horse is at the bridge,
The second bridge below the ferry house:
Why do you tarry? Can your ears not hear
This dreadful bell, whose every ringing stroke
Robs one brief minute from your boyish life.
Go quickly.

GUIDO.
Ay! he will come soon enough.

DUCHESS.
Who?

GUIDO.
[calmly]
Why, the HEADSMAN.

DUCHESS.
No, no.

GUIDO.
Only he
Can bring me out of Padua.

DUCHESS.
You dare not!
You dare not burden my o'erburdened soul
With two dead men! I think one is enough.
For when I stand before God, face to face,
I would not have you, with a scarlet thread
Around your white throat, coming up behind
To say I did it.

GUIDO.
Madam, I wait.

DUCHESS.
No, no, you cannot: you do not understand,
I have less power in Padua to-night
Than any common woman; they will kill you.
I saw the scaffold as I crossed the square,
Already the low rabble throng about it
With fearful jests, and horrid merriment,
As though it were a morris-dancer's platform,
And not Death's sable throne. O Guido, Guido,
You must escape!

GUIDO.
Madam, I tarry here.

DUCHESS.
Guido, you shall not: it would be a thing
So terrible that the amazed stars
Would fall from heaven, and the palsied moon
Be in her sphere eclipsed, and the great sun
Refuse to shine upon the unjust earth
Which saw thee die.

GUIDO.
Be sure I shall not stir.

DUCHESS.
[wringing her hands]
Is one sin not enough, but must it breed
A second sin more horrible again
Than was the one that bare it? O God, God,
Seal up sin's teeming womb, and make it barren,
I will not have more blood upon my hand
Than I have now.

GUIDO.
[seizing her hand]
What! am I fallen so low
That I may not have leave to die for you?

DUCHESS.
[tearing her hand away]
Die for me? no, my life is a vile thing,
Thrown to the miry highways of this world;
You shall not die for me, you shall not, Guido;
I am a guilty woman.

GUIDO.
Guilty? let those

Who know what a thing temptation is,
Let those who have not walked as we have done,
In the red fire of passion, those whose lives
Are dull and colourless, in a word let those,
If any such there be, who have not loved,
Cast stones against you. As for me -

DUCHESS.
Alas!

GUIDO.
[falling at her feet]
You are my lady, and you are my love!
O hair of gold, O crimson lips, O face
Made for the luring and the love of man!
Incarnate image of pure loveliness!
Worshipping thee I do forget the past,
Worshipping thee my soul comes close to thine,
Worshipping thee I seem to be a god,
And though they give my body to the block,
Yet is my love eternal!
[DUCHESS puts her hands over her face: GUIDO draws them down.]
Sweet, lift up
The trailing curtains that overhang your eyes
That I may look into those eyes, and tell you
I love you, never more than now when Death
Thrusts his cold lips between us: Beatrice,
I love you: have you no word left to say?
Oh, I can bear the executioner,
But not this silence: will you not say you love me?
Speak but that word and Death shall lose his sting,
But speak it not, and fifty thousand deaths
Are, in comparison, mercy. Oh, you are cruel,
And do not love me.

DUCHESS.
Alas! I have no right
For I have stained the innocent hands of love
With spilt-out blood: there is blood on the ground;
I set it there.

GUIDO.
Sweet, it was not yourself,
It was some devil tempted you.

DUCHESS.
[rising suddenly]
No, no,
We are each our own devil, and we make
This world our hell.

GUIDO.

Then let high Paradise
Fall into Tartarus! for I shall make
This world my heaven for a little space.
The sin was mine, if any sin there was.
'Twas I who nurtured murder in my heart,
Sweetened my meats, seasoned my wine with it,
And in my fancy slew the accursed DUKE
A hundred times a day. Why, had this man
Died half so often as I wished him to,
Death had been stalking ever through the house,
And murder had not slept.
But you, fond heart,
Whose little eyes grew tender over a whipt hound,
You whom the little children laughed to see
Because you brought the sunlight where you passed,
You the white angel of God's purity,
This which men call your sin, what was it?

DUCHESS.

Ay!
What was it? There are times it seems a dream,
An evil dream sent by an evil god,
And then I see the dead face in the coffin
And know it is no dream, but that my hand
Is red with blood, and that my desperate soul
Striving to find some haven for its love
From the wild tempest of this raging world,
Has wrecked its bark upon the rocks of sin.
What was it, said you? murder merely? Nothing
But murder, horrible murder.

GUIDO.

Nay, nay, nay,
'Twas but the passion-flower of your love
That in one moment leapt to terrible life,
And in one moment bare this gory fruit,
Which I had plucked in thought a thousand times.
My soul was murderous, but my hand refused;
Your hand wrought murder, but your soul was pure.
And so I love you, Beatrice, and let him
Who has no mercy for your stricken head,
Lack mercy up in heaven! Kiss me, sweet.
[Tries to kiss her.]

DUCHESS.

No, no, your lips are pure, and mine are soiled,
For Guilt has been my paramour, and Sin
Lain in my bed: O Guido, if you love me
Get hence, for every moment is a worm
Which gnaws your life away: nay, sweet, get hence,

And if in after time you think of me,
Think of me as of one who loved you more
Than anything on earth; think of me, Guido,
As of a woman merely, one who tried
To make her life a sacrifice to love,
And slew love in the trial: Oh, what is that?
The bell has stopped from ringing, and I hear
The feet of armed men upon the stair.

GUIDO.
[aside]
That is the signal for the guard to come.

DUCHESS.
Why has the bell stopped ringing?

GUIDO.
If you must know,
That stops my life on this side of the grave,
But on the other we shall meet again.

DUCHESS.
No, no, 'tis not too late: you must get hence;
The horse is by the bridge, there is still time.
Away, away, you must not tarry here!
[Noise of Soldiers in the passage.]

A VOICE OUTSIDE
Room for the LORD JUSTICE of Padua!
[The LORD JUSTICE is seen through the grated window passing down
the corridor preceded by men bearing torches.]

DUCHESS.
It is too late.

A VOICE OUTSIDE
Room for the HEADSMAN.

DUCHESS.
[sinks down]
Oh!
[The HEADSMAN with his axe on his shoulder is seen passing the
corridor, followed by Monks bearing candles.]

GUIDO.
Farewell, dear love, for I must drink this poison.
I do not fear the HEADSMAN, but I would die
Not on the lonely scaffold.
But here,
Here in thine arms, kissing thy mouth: farewell!
[Goes to the table and takes the goblet up.] What, art thou empty?

[Throws it to the ground.]
O thou churlish gaoler,
Even of poisons niggard!

DUCHESS.
[faintly]
Blame him not.

GUIDO.
O God! you have not drunk it, Beatrice?
Tell me you have not?

DUCHESS.
Were I to deny it,
There is a fire eating at my heart
Which would find utterance.

GUIDO.
O treacherous love,
Why have you not left a drop for me?

DUCHESS.
No, no, it held but death enough for one.

GUIDO.
Is there no poison still upon your lips,
That I may draw it from them?

DUCHESS.
Why should you die?
You have not spilt blood, and so need not die:
I have spilt blood, and therefore I must die.
Was it not said blood should be spilt for blood?
Who said that? I forget.

GUIDO.
Tarry for me,
Our souls will go together.

DUCHESS.
Nay, you must live.
There are many other women in the world
Who will love you, and not murder for your sake.

GUIDO.
I love you only.

DUCHESS.
You need not die for that.

GUIDO.
Ah, if we die together, love, why then
Can we not lie together in one grave?

DUCHESS.
A grave is but a narrow wedding-bed.

GUIDO.
It is enough for us

DUCHESS.
And they will strew it
With a stark winding-sheet, and bitter herbs:
I think there are no roses in the grave,
Or if there are, they all are withered now
Since my Lord went there.

GUIDO.
Ah! dear Beatrice,
Your lips are roses that death cannot wither.

DUCHESS.
Nay, if we lie together, will not my lips
Fall into dust, and your enamoured eyes
Shrivel to sightless sockets, and the worms,
Which are our groomsmen, eat away your heart?

GUIDO.
I do not care: Death has no power on love.
And so by Love's immortal sovereignty
I will die with you.

DUCHESS.
But the grave is black,
And the pit black, so I must go before
To light the candles for your coming hither.
No, no, I will not die, I will not die.
Love, you are strong, and young, and very brave;
Stand between me and the angel of death,
And wrestle with him for me.
[Thrusts GUIDO in front of her with his back to the audience.]
I will kiss you,
When you have thrown him. Oh, have you no cordial,
To stay the workings of this poison in me?
Are there no rivers left in Italy
That you will not fetch me one cup of water
To quench this fire?

GUIDO.
O God!

DUCHESS.
You did not tell me
There was a drought in Italy, and no water:
Nothing but fire.

GUIDO.
O Love!

DUCHESS.
Send for a leech,
Not him who stanched my husband, but another
We have no time: send for a leech, I say:
There is an antidote against each poison,
And he will sell it if we give him money.
Tell him that I will give him Padua,
For one short hour of life: I will not die.
Oh, I am sick to death; no, do not touch me,
This poison gnaws my heart: I did not know
It was such pain to die: I thought that life
Had taken all the agonies to itself;
It seems it is not so.

GUIDO.
O damned stars
Quench your vile cresset-lights in tears, and bid
The moon, your mistress, shine no more to-night.

DUCHESS.
Guido, why are we here? I think this room
Is poorly furnished for a marriage chamber.
Let us get hence at once. Where are the horses?
We should be on our way to Venice now.
How cold the night is! We must ride faster.
[The Monks begin to chant outside.]
Music! It should be merrier; but grief
Is of the fashion now, I know not why.
You must not weep: do we not love each other? -
That is enough. Death, what do you here?
You were not bidden to this table, sir;
Away, we have no need of you: I tell you
It was in wine I pledged you, not in poison.
They lied who told you that I drank your poison.
It was spilt upon the ground, like my Lord's blood;
You came too late.

GUIDO.
Sweet, there is nothing there:
These things are only unreal shadows.

DUCHESS.
Death,

Why do you tarry, get to the upper chamber;
The cold meats of my husband's funeral feast
Are set for you; this is a wedding feast.
You are out of place, sir; and, besides, 'tis summer.
We do not need these heavy fires now,
You scorch us.
Oh, I am burned up,
Can you do nothing? Water, give me water,
Or else more poison. No: I feel no pain -
Is it not curious I should feel no pain? -
And Death has gone away, I am glad of that.
I thought he meant to part us. Tell me, Guido,
Are you not sorry that you ever saw me?

GUIDO.
I swear I would not have lived otherwise.
Why, in this dull and common world of ours
Men have died looking for such moments as this
And have not found them.

DUCHESS.
Then you are not sorry?
How strange that seems.

GUIDO.
What, Beatrice, have I not
Stood face to face with beauty? That is enough
For one man's life. Why, love, I could be merry;
I have been often sadder at a feast,
But who were sad at such a feast as this
When Love and Death are both our cup-bearers?
We love and die together.

DUCHESS.
Oh, I have been
Guilty beyond all women, and indeed
Beyond all women punished. Do you think -
No, that could not be. Oh, do you think that love
Can wipe the bloody stain from off my hands,
Pour balm into my wounds, heal up my hurts,
And wash my scarlet sins as white as snow? -
For I have sinned.

GUIDO.
They do not sin at all
Who sin for love.

DUCHESS.
No, I have sinned, and yet
Perchance my sin will be forgiven me.
I have loved much

[They kiss each other now for the first time in this Act, when
suddenly the DUCHESS leaps up in the dreadful spasm of death, tears
in agony at her dress, and finally, with face twisted and distorted
with pain, falls back dead in a chair. GUIDO seizing her dagger
from her belt, kills himself; and, as he falls across her knees,
clutches at the cloak which is on the back of the chair, and throws
it entirely over her. There is a little pause. Then down the
passage comes the tramp of Soldiers; the door is opened, and the
LORD JUSTICE, the HEADSMAN, and the Guard enter and see this figure
shrouded in black, and GUIDO lying dead across her. The LORD
JUSTICE rushes forward and drags the cloak off the DUCHESS, whose
face is now the marble image of peace, the sign of God's
forgiveness.]

Tableau

CURTAIN

Oscar Wilde (1854-1900)

Oscar Wilde was an Irish poet, fiction writer and playwright who had a very special life story that made him become considered by many as a sort of martyr of freedom and literature. He had become England's most popular and controversial playwright in the 1880s before he got involved in a court trial in which he was proved guilty of homosexuality, which was a serious crime in Victorian England. After spending two years in prison, an experience that made his psychological and physical health deteriorate, he left the country to seek exile in France and soon died there. Today he is mainly remembered for his fictional masterpiece *The Picture of Dorian Gray* (1890) and also for his dramatic masterpiece *The Importance of Being Earnest* (1895).

Oscar Wilde was born to well-off and intellectual parents in the city of Dublin and received a decent education in which he had always been a distinguished student. His mother Jane Wilde was herself renowned in Ireland as a refined poet. As for Oscar's father, Sir William Wilde, he was a humanitarian medical doctor and a surgeon who left important works of medicine and archeology. Today, he is remembered as one of Ireland's greatest men of science. From an early age, Oscar Wilde became fluent in French and German and then mastered classical schools of philosophy. After an experience at Magdalen College in Oxford, he adopted the philosophical school of aestheticism to become one of its most famous proponents.

After graduation, Wilde's writing activities multiplied. While preaching among literary circles his very famous slogan "Art for art's sake," which objects to all sorts of politicization or moralization of art and literature, he wrote and published collections of poems and short stories. In 1878, Wilde's poem "Ravenna" had made him win the Newdigate Prize. Oscar's first collection of poems was published in 1881 under the title *Poems* and received considerable attention from critics.

He married Constance Llyod in 1884 to have two sons, Cyril and Vyvyan. Constance came from an even wealthier family than his and used to support him, to fund his publications and even to send him money for his personal subsistence at the moments of hardship that characterized his twilight years. Starting from 1882, Wilde lectured in different countries including Ireland, England, Canada and the United States. When he was visiting the latter, his trip was prolonged more than once thanks to the success of his lectures and his published works.

In 1888, Wilde published *The Happy Prince and Other Stories* to be followed by *Lord Arthur Savile's Crime and Other Stories* in 1891. Wilde's short stories were mainly fairy tales for children (originally for his own children), but they can also be enjoyable and instructive for adults. Apart from that, Wilde also started publishing essays and magazine articles for *The Pall Mall Gazette* and *The Woman's World* to serve as the editor of the latter for a number of years.

It was in *Lippincott's Monthly Magazine* that his only novel *The Picture of Dorian Gray* was first published in 1890 to face strong resistance by critics who raised controversies over its homoerotic insinuations. Generally, the story adopts fantastic effects and deals with the theme of the Faustian pact. Dorian is a young man who, after seeing a painting of himself done by a renowned painter, falls in love with it and wishes his youthful beauty depicted in the painting lasts forever. A magical bargain is achieved through which Dorian will physically remain the same while the painting itself will age. Thus, he engages in a life of pleasure and libertinage not caring about age. He is, however, depressed by the mere look at his own aging reflection in the picture as it becomes uglier and uglier. By the end of the novel, he takes a knife and stabs the canvas to kill only himself. Despite the diatribe that some critics launched against the novel's explicit "immorality" and "homosexual allusions," *The Picture of Dorian Gray* has become considered as a refined masterpiece, mainly posthumously in the twentieth century.

The reaction of critics made Wilde even write more essays to explain his artistic vision of aestheticism and to further explain his position according to which art should be considered as only a manifestation of beauty that does not tolerate any moral or political evaluation of the artistic act. In fact, all sorts of moral judgment of art are irrelevant according to Wilde. For him, art is an individualistic act of constant improvisation that should always remain free of all moral and social shackles. The question of whether literature and art in general should take up a moral, social or political role is still debated by today's literary and philosophical circles. During this period, Wilde also wrote other essays on the philosophy of art and politics as well as biographies.

After the publication of the novel, Wilde's plays followed to make him more popular than ever before. His first play was first written in French under the title *Salomé* (1891). It was followed by *Lady Windermere's Fan* in 1892, *A Woman of No Importance* in 1893, *An Ideal Husband* in 1895 and *The Importance of Being Earnest* in the same year. Most of these plays were social comedies or comedies of manners that painted the Victorian society, parodied and satirized its manners, etiquette and social hypocrisy. Wilde's plays, which remained on stages for long and enabled the author to make considerable fortunes, served as a mirror that made the Victorian audience laugh at the contradictions and paradoxes in which they found themselves. The dialogues were stuffed with witty remarks, humorous misunderstandings and sharp quips that could only inspire appreciation among the people that they criticized. Wilde had still to face the dissatisfaction of Victorian diehard conservatives, though.

By that time, Wilde was constantly moving between Paris and London where he attended his premières and frequented literary salons. Unfortunately, the 1890s did not only bring fame and financial prosperity to Oscar Wilde, but also much trouble that would ultimately ruin him. All started when he made acquaintance with young Alfred Douglas in 1891. They engaged in an adventurous homosexual relationship, a relationship that was suspected by Alfred's atheist yet conservative father, the Marquis of Queensberry.

Wilde's relationship with Douglas was romantic and biographers note that the prosperous rising star used to pamper his partner, realizing all his dreams. Though much younger than the celebrated playwright, it was Douglas who introduced Wilde to the world of male debauchery and prostitution. Meanwhile, Douglas's father was haunting the couple, trying to find out about their secret. When he finally became sure of the affair, he explicitly threatened Wilde.

The Marquis of Queensberry had never thought of suing Wilde, however, was it not for the fact that Wilde himself started by prosecuting him. The story began when Queensberry defamed Wilde among his circles by describing him as a homosexual and a sodomite. Wilde's mistake was to prosecute Queensberry for libel while he knew that it was very easy to find proofs of his homosexual behavior and that this was criminalized by British law. During trial, Queensberry's lawyers were trying to prove that their client's claims were founded in order to absolve him from the accusation of libel. They finally succeeded in their mission. Right after the end of the trial, a warrant was issued for Wilde's arrest, his crime being "gross indecency".

Having lost a lot of money on the trial and lawyers, Wilde had also to pay all Queensberry's expenses before he was sentenced to a two-year imprisonment with hard labor. The experience of prison gravely affected him both psychologically and physically. Despite the time and idleness that prison usually offers, his literary activity decreased greatly. In fact, he only succeeded in finishing one work while in prison. This work was intended to be a letter to Douglas that Wilde entitled *De Profundis* (Latin for "from the depths"). The long letter, which was later published in book form to become among Wilde's most read works, spoke about the author's experience during the trials. The letter also displayed a feeling of remorse. Wilde claimed that his mistake was that he had wished to experience all sorts of earthly pleasure when pleasure had wrongly been the sole purpose of his life.

Wilde even developed religious sentiments in prison and wished to have a retreat at the Catholic Church after being released, yet this was not accepted. When he left the prison in 1897, he immediately decided to leave the country for France where he lived almost alone after having lost his money and the luster of fame. He was only frequented by a small number of intimate friends and received money for subsistence from his wife, though they were officially separated. In Paris, Wilde wrote his last work before he passed away. This was a long poem entitled *The Ballad of Reading Gaol*. The verse recounts the horrors of prison.

On November 30th, 1900, Oscar Wilde died of cerebral meningitis in the French capital. He rests today at the Père Lachaise Cemetery where he is visited by thousands of his readers and fans every year. Today, as misconceptions about Wilde's life and personal choices have changed, his works as well as his career have helped raise him to the status of legends.

www.ingramcontent.com/pod-product-compliance
Lightning Source LLC
Chambersburg PA
CBHW071414170626
46811CB00003B/1405